AFRICAN WRITERS SERIES

The Marabi Dance

MODIKWE DIKOBE

The Marabi Dance

HEINEMANN

Heinemann International Literature and Textbooks
a division of Heinemann Educational Books Ltd
Halley Court, Jordan Hill, Oxford OX2 8EJ

Heinemann Educational Books Inc.
361 Hanover Street, Portsmouth, New Hampshire, 03801, USA

Heinemann Educational Books (Nigeria) Ltd
PMB 5205, Ibadan
Heinemann Educational Boleswa
PO Box 10103, Village Post Office, Gaborone, Botswana

LONDON EDINBURGH MELBOURNE
SYDNEY AUCKLAND SINGAPORE TOKYO
PARIS MADRID ATHENS BOLOGNA

Series Editor: Adewale Maja-Pearce

ISBN 0-435-90124-9

Printed in Great Britain by
Cox & Wyman Ltd, Reading, Berkshire

93 94 15 14 13 12 11 10 9

Thanks

Much revision of the original manuscript of *The Marabi Dance* was necessary in order to make the author's intention clear, though the light of that intention showed vividly from the first. Mr N. Levy and the late Valerie Phillip did the main editorial work. Useful questions and suggestions, encouragement and practical aid in producing a presentable typescript came from Professor Guy Butler, Professor Monica Wilson and Mr and Mrs Don Maclennan. Mr Lionel Abrahams has associated himself with the fate of this novel over a number of years and he joins Mr Dikobe in expressing deep gratitude to all who have helped.

Dedication

I was born in the year 1913, in the Northern Transvaal. When I was ten I went with my parents to live in Sophiatown and Doornfontein, in Johannesburg. This book is written for my former schoolmates at the Albert Street School. Someone like Martha may still be alive, and her son may be one of those young men now being harassed by the pass laws, endorsed out of the cities and made strangers in the land of their birth.

1

THE MOLEFE YARD, where Martha lived, was also home to more than twenty other people. It served a row of five rooms, each about fourteen by twelve feet in size. When it rained, the yard was as muddy as a cattle kraal, and the smell of beer, thrown out by the police on their raids, combining with the stench of the lavatories, was nauseating.

The beer business was mostly done on Sundays for the benefit of the domestic workers. The skokiaan enabled the men to fight more bravely in the Amalaita boxing bouts. Those with stronger heads drank methylated spirits.

The visitors on Sundays swarmed like bees in the yards and streets of Doornfontein. They stood in groups, talking loudly, greeting each other, shaking hands, kissing on the pretext that they were sisters and brothers. The drinking parties sat in the houses, the men singing as loudly as their throats would allow, swaying like tree branches in the fumes of liquor and tobacco. The men patted the women on the buttocks and made love to mothers and their daughters. At night the children pretended to be fast asleep by covering their heads with blankets and snoring.

This was where Martha grew up.

She attended the Albert Street School, part of St. Paul's Methodist Church. The church was built to serve the African community in the area, the school was for their children. She sat for Standard Five, then her parents withdrew her from school because she'd been going out with boys, and they considered the fees to be a waste of money.

She'd been popular at her school. Her sturdy figure had added to the attraction of her round baritone voice. When she had taken part with the boys in the singing she had been treated as one of their own sex, and the girls had much awe and respect for her. When it was learned that she would not return to school, her classmates and teacher were dismayed. They blamed a boy at the American Board School for the misdemeanour she was supposed to have committed.

There were more absentees on Mondays than any other day of the week. The apology often given was, 'I had to go to fetch the washing for my mother.' But on this particular Monday, when the register was called, a girl living in the same yard as Martha said she would not ever be coming to school any more. The teacher was stunned. When the girl was asked why this was so, she simply shrugged her shoulders and sat down. The expression on her face indicated the reason for Martha's withdrawal from school, and the teacher and the children were not slow to read it.

At the end of the school day, the class teacher reported Martha's absence to the Head.

'I have seen her in the company of a Marabi boy, called George. It is probable that her parents have decided to withdraw her from school before it is noticed,' said the Head.

'I am very sorry to lose the girl. Though she was not bright in her work she was the best in the Senior Choir and it was through her efforts that the school won the Eisteddfod Cup from St Cyprian School last year.'

'Go and find out from her parents why she is being kept away from school. If you find out that she has been seduced by that American Board School boy, we will take up the case for them,' said the Head.

'The girl would make a living from singing if she received a proper training. I have been wondering if we could introduce her to Mr Samson.' The teacher was truly concerned and resolved to do his best to help the girl.

The Head was right in guessing that Martha's withdrawal from school had something to do with George. He was the pianist at the Marabi parties run by Ma-Ndlovu which were very popular but not favoured by respectable people. They knew Marabi as a dance party for persons of a 'low type' and for 'malala-pipe', pipe-sleepers, homeless ruffian children.

How Ma-Ndlovu became a Marabi queen was as follows.

Ma-Ndlovu had come from Zululand in search of her young husband Vuzi who had left her when she was three months pregnant. She had borne him a baby girl and waited three years before venturing to look for him. She had heard that he was living with another woman at Prospect Township and she arrived with her daughter at the station early one afternoon. She hired a ricksha to take her to a house in the township. After paying the ricksha puller, she pleaded with him to wait until she had been admitted to the house.

She went to the door and knocked. 'Ngena – come in,' answered a voice from inside.

Ma-Ndlovu hesitated and tightly fastened the cloth that tied her baby to her back. A woman came to the door and told her to come inside instead of waiting outside like a witch hypnotized by medicines. She went in and waited to be greeted.

'Hau mfazi, you come into my house and do not greet me!'

Ma-Ndlovu explained that she was a Zulu and it was not her custom to greet first. At this a man stepped in without knocking and sat on a hard bench near the bed.

'Baba, Baba,' cried the child of the house.

'Go to your father,' said the woman to the child.

He took the child from her and placed it on his lap. The child kissed its father and began searching his pockets for sweets.

'Baba, apé ama sweet.'

The man fumbled from one pocket to another and produced a brown paper packet.

2

Only then Vuzi Madonda recognised his first wife. He was stunned and greeted her in a feeble voice: 'Sakubona Ma-Ndlovu.'

'Sakubona Baba ica Tandi – Greetings, father of Tandi.'

The woman of the house breathed heavily and stared in puzzlement at her husband and the strange woman.

'Ma-Khumalo!' the man said to her, 'this woman is my wife from Zululand.' The look on Ma-Khumalo's face changed from curiosity to anger, from anger to bewilderment. From the movement of her thick lips she appeared to be muttering something but it was impossible to hear what she was saying. Then she walked across to Vuzi, picked up her child and left the room without saying a word.

Vuzi and Ma-Ndlovu sat watching each other unspeaking until the silence was broken by a complaint from Tandi.

'Why have you come here without telling me?' demanded Vuzi.

'How could I tell you when you have not been writing or sending money?'

The man left the house and returned a little later with a loaf of bread and a bottle of cool drink and gave them to his wife. She broke the bread with her hands and handed a big piece to the child and let it drink from the bottle. When the child had done with the bottle, she took it and drank from it herself.

'I must find you a place to sleep,' said Vuzi. He left the room and was heard speaking to a neighbour who lived a few doors away. A few minutes later this woman entered the room and greeted Ma-Ndlovu.

'Come with me, mfazi.' Ma-Ndlovu followed the neighbour in silence. When they had entered her room, she asked if they had eaten. On hearing what they had had, she brought a plate of hard porridge and meat and looked on while they ate.

Ma-Khumalo returned to Vuzi's house after an hour's absence with two men and several women. The men carried sticks and the women wore heavy rugs over their heads.

'Madonda, we have come to inquire why you have brought another woman into this house.' The voice was that of one of the men.

'The woman who has come tonight,' answered Madonda, 'is my wife from Zululand. I told Ma-Khumalo that I had a wife at home. I have not chased Ma-Khumalo out.'

'You are a liar!' snapped Ma-Khumalo and threatened to land a blow on Madonda's head.

'Madonda,' Madonda appealed to the men, 'if you cannot control this woman, please get out and take her away with you before I smash your heads to bits!' He got up from his chair and brandished three sticks which he seized from the table. Ma-Khumalo, knowing his temper and courage, entreated him to be calm.

'Hau Baba! Hau Baba,' she implored.

'Puma! Puma! Out!' cried Madonda in a fury.

3

The women pleaded with the men to leave, and tried to explain that Ma-Khumalo did not know that the woman was his wife from Zululand. 'She will not object to her remaining in the house.'

Ma-Ndlovu and her hostess in the nearby room heard all that was said in the house.

'Umadoda ezi nja – men are dogs,' said her hostess. Ma-Ndlovu nodded and smiled.

The women tried as best they could to live together as wives of the one man. They cooked alternately and washed for him, but Ma-Khumalo made it impossible for Ma-Ndlovu to share a bed with him. She told her friends that Ma-Ndlovu, a 'nodindwa', which means a prostitute, would never sleep with Madonda. Whenever Ma-Ndlovu went out in the evening and Madonda followed, she also came out and demanded to know what they were about so late at night.

After many months of living together, Ma-Ndlovu learnt some of the ways in which the location women made money without the knowledge of their husbands. Instead of being gloomy and unhappy she became radiant and bright, and her husband became jealous and threatened to send her back home. But Ma-Ndlovu took no heed of his threats. One evening when Madonda returned from work he found that Ma-Ndlovu and the child were not at home. He inquired from Ma-Khumalo where she had gone to.

'I don't know what she does. You paid a lot of cattle for her and for me you paid nothing! Ha-ha! Your good wife of the kraal! We of the towns are bad and prostitutes! Go and find her yourself.'

Madonda asked the woman with whom Ma-Ndlovu had spent the first days of her arrival if she knew where she had gone.

'She said she had been promised work somewhere in the mine quarters and that she was going to take the work even if she was not well paid. She would not be treated like a virgin by her own husband from whom she had learned to be a woman. She said you could remain with your town wife.'

So Ma-Ndlovu worked in the mine quarters and sold beer in the evening in the mine dumps. It was here that she met a Portuguese East African mine worker and made love to him. She introduced him to her employer as her husband. On some occasions, Alberto came to sleep on the premises and worked in the garden at the weekends and helped to clean the windows. He accompanied her to the mine dumps to sell beer and stood guard against any untoward events. They returned late in the evening to count the money they made and hid it under the mattress. Alberto gave his monthly wages and brought the child Tandi dresses from the concession store.

Ma-Ndlovu's employers loved Tandi and taught her to speak English and Afrikaans. After a few months' practice; she could speak better than

4

her mother. 'Ma, kom hier,' she would summon her in Afrikaans: 'I don't like jam,' she would say.

They both saved money in the Post Office and sent money home to their parents when they felt it was necessary.

'Hau! nge fumene indoda – I have found a man,' Ma-Ndlovu boasted to other women.

A few months later the mine closed, and Mr and Mrs Reenen and their children were very sorry to part with Tandi and her mother. They bought dolls and dresses, and shoes and a picture book.

Alberto went to look for a room in Prospect Township and when he found one he moved his 'wife' and 'child' to their new location home. Their room was a few streets away from Madonda's house and Ma-Ndlovu made up her mind that she would never allow him to interfere with her new husband. Alberto had made many friends on the mines and they would come to her aid if any trouble arose.

'Ama-Russia asoku lungisa – the Russians* will fix him!' Alberto told her.

The blanketed men from Basutoland were her beer customers and the Shangaans from her husband's home brought her mine rations and called her 'Mama'.

Alberto's contract of service with the mines expired. If he wished, he could renew the contract for a further three years, as he had done in the past, or leave the mines and continue as a Fah-fee runner for a Chinaman. He made easy money from his commissions, and a promise of a weekly allowance from the Chinaman enabled him to refuse a fourth contract with the mines. His new employer had him registered with the Pass Office as a domestic worker. He learned the art of dealing with the police and discovered how to slip through their cordons. If he was caught, Mr Pin would bail him out or pay a fine so as to avoid a court hearing.

Alberto and Ma-Ndlovu became popular through selling beer and running Marabi Dances and Fah-fee games. They were respected by many as wealthy and peaceful people.

George had been playing the piano at a Marabi Dance from the Saturday night to the following Sunday afternoon. Martha had come to watch him and sing with him early on the Sunday morning, and now was tired and resting on a paraffin tin beside him.

George had been engaged to play the piano for the two days by Auntie Ma-Ndlovu. The drinks, skokiaan and other concoctions, were sold in a room adjoining the one in which the Marabi Dance was held. She rented

* A group of gangsters operating in the Johannesburg non-White Townships were called 'Russians'. They were always Basutos, and usually mine workers.

5

yet another room where brandy was sold. This room was furnished, and she and Alberto lived there.

Ma-Ndlovu's beer and dance party was drawing to a close. Martha looked pensively at George, his fingers stretched like cobwebs over the keys of the piano. George played the last tune and then stopped as the dancers began to leave the house. Soon all was as quiet as if nothing had ever taken place in the room. All that remained of the party was the dust kicked up by the dancers and the stench and heat of the room.

'I have made twelve pounds ten shillings from the dance, five pounds from the skokiaan and ten guineas from the brandy. How much have you made from the Fah-fee, Alberto?' asked Ma-Ndlovu.

'The Chinaman is bankrupt!' exclaimed Alberto. 'Mrs Moremi bet heavily and caught "white woman". So the Chinaman could not pay. All our money is gone.' Alberto waved his arms to indicate how the money had vanished.

Ma-Ndlovu planned another big party. She offered to pay Martha to sing to George's accompaniment during the whole party. Martha knew she would never get the agreement of her father and mother and was afraid to accept, but George, knowing how her heart beat for him, accused her of not wanting to sing with him. When she denied this, he urged her to prove it. It would mean staying out all night, but Martha could not resist George. Perhaps his urgency was a sign that he really did care for her, not only for her singing and her body. At last she agreed to perform during the whole Marabi Dance party.

Ma-Ndlovu ordered a great many bottles of brandy from a white liquor runner to whom she paid an extra shilling for each bottle that was bought. She prepared ten gallons of beer and brewed her several concoctions. A large quantity of meat was bought which she cooked with vegetables. When she had done her cooking she made a special visit to George to ask him to play the latest hits. Martha sang:

Tjeka-Tjeka messie.
Tjeka-Tjeka sebebe.
Tjeka ngoanyane,
Tjeka-Tjeka ngoam wa Marabi . . .

Give give, girl.
Give give, prostitute.
Give girl,
Give, give, girl of the Marabi . . .

The dancers swayed from side to side like mealie stalks; the right and left feet moving forward and back like springbok crossing a river. They sang as loudly as they could, singing for joy to the spirits of their forefathers. George ran his short fingers over the black and white keyboard as if they were moved by an electric charge. He sang with his face pitched to the ceiling. Martha moved like a cocopan full of mine sand turning at an intersection. Her round female baritone voice filled the hall and made it vibrate with sound. The flies, which had become a nuisance to the dancers, buzzed in harmony, and the rats and mice between the wall and the false front of the hall, scrambled into the ceiling.

Ma-Ndlovu served the brandy drinkers, humming the tunes that were being sung inside the hall. As she moved, she danced with her dress spread out and showed her pretty petticoat. The brandy drinkers ordered half-jack quantities, paid a pound and refused the change. They drank and sang, swaying on the chairs as train coaches sway between the stations of Langlaagte and Croesus. Sometimes they fell and landed on their faces, sleeping where they had fallen.

Suddenly there was confusion in the hall. A man had rushed in and spoken to Ma-Ndlovu. She started screaming.

'Yoo oooo, youlele Indoda yama! – she has killed my husband!'

'Ehe, Ma-Ndlovu? What is it?' asked the astonished crowd.

'Madonda, my husband, has been killed by a motor car. He has been bewitched by Ma-Khumalo. Yoooooo, indoda yomtshato – my husband who has paid lobola for me.'

There was pandemonium everywhere. The beer drinkers, who had ordered a four gallon can of beer before paying, began collecting for the dead and paid for the beer. The youngsters who had been dancing ran home and told their parents about the tragedy that had befallen Ma-Ndlovu. Then a home which, only a short while before, had been agog fell into a deathly silence. The noisy, excited dancers and children dispersed, and those who had been patronizing the beer party stood outside perplexed. They had seen Alberto, whom they regarded as Ma-Ndlovu's husband, only a few moments ago. George and Martha lingered a while, hoping to be paid. But when the neighbours began trickling in to inquire about the death, they left.

Alberto, on hearing his wife cry for a husband with whom she'd not been living for ten years, took counsel from the mineworkers and was advised to stay away from the vigil and the funeral.

Ma-Ndlovu appeared grief-stricken. She was taken to Madonda's uncle who lived in a municipal compound.

'I have come to you, Uncle, about the death of my husband, Vuzi. He paid a lot of cattle for me, while he paid nothing for Ma-Khumalo. She is only a nodindwa. I must have my husband's head. You, Uncle, have all the power to let the white people give you his corpse.'

Uncle Madonda thought for a long time before giving his decision and finally agreed to have the body taken to Ma-Ndlovu's house instead of Ma-Khumalo's.

The corpse was kept in the government mortuary until Saturday. Arrangements were made for the funeral and the week of vigils that was to precede it. For the funeral, buses would be chartered to enable Ma-Ndlovu's friends to pay their last respects to her husband. On the day the corpse was brought to the house hundreds of people came to the vigil and placed half-crowns and ten-shilling and pound notes upon the tables that had been laid out for collection in the hall and the rooms of neighbours and friends. Night after night the vigil was held. Men and women sang and preached:

> Umuzi ukhona a Zulwini.
> Ungangwa ziziqhwaga kuphela.

> There is a city beyond
> Entered only by the brave.

They preached that that city is only entered by those who believe in God the Father and the Son and the Holy Ghost.

Ma-Ndlovu sat sadly at the head of the deceased. She was wrapped in a heavy rug and had a tin of beer beside her. Now and then she scooped some from the tin with a mug and gulped a mouthful.

Ma-Khumalo sat in solemnity and melancholy at the late Vuzi's feet and murmured inaudible words. Uncle Madonda sat with a group of men outside around a big fire where the liver and offal of an ox, slaughtered to appease Madonda's spirits, was being roasted.

George, on the way home after Ma-Ndlovu's interrupted Marabi party, told Martha how upset he was. He had played so well and helped Ma-Ndlovu to make a lot of money and then to hear that her husband had died! He took Martha as far as the gate of the Molefe Yard and kissed her goodnight before returning to his home in Greenie Street, City and Suburbs. He told his mother of the death of Ma-Ndlovu's husband and why he had no money for the rent collector whom she had promised to pay on the following Monday.

'Here's food, George – eat. You must be very hungry and tired.'

'No thanks, Ma. I don't want to eat.'

'George, my child, town people make money from dead bodies. They keep the bodies for longer than a week in order to get more people to collect money from. Women claim husbands from whom they have been parted for years. Not because they loved them but to disgrace the women with whom they had been living.

'Ma-Ndlovu has robbed you by not paying you, my son, but the spirits of your forefathers will revenge you! Hau! I am going to send her Mafu-funyane, the madness that causes one to see chimpanzees, before her husband is lowered into his grave.'

After George had left her, Martha walked through the main gate of the Molefe Yard. She noticed a group of children clustered around a brazier fire in front of one of the corrugated walled rooms. The light was off and

8

the occupants appeared to be asleep. When the children saw Martha they spoke in low but audible voices. 'It's ausi (big sister) Moipone!'

'Modimo!' one called at her, 'your mother and father have been looking for you since Saturday.' They laughed loudly when she came nearer and the one who had addressed her ran away into the lavatory and closed the door. The others pretended not to have heard what had been said and hung their heads and giggled inwardly.

Martha drew nearer and asked what the girl, Tiny, was laughing at. She pushed the lavatory door open and dragged her out and gave her a good smack. The little girl pretended to cry and covered her face with her arms and went through the motions of wiping away the tears.

The whole yard seemed to be asleep, except for the children, who for some reason had not yet gone to bed. Martha reached the cottage common door and as she pushed it open the stench of breath came to her nostrils. It was dark in the passage. Only the sound of snoring could be heard, then the floorboards creaked audibly under her feet. Her heart throbbed for fear of arousing the sleepers. She wished the door would miraculously open of itself and that she could spread her blankets and slip into them without being seen or heard. She pressed her ear to the door. Her father was snoring heavily, and another snore like a frog croaking was heard next door. She was pleased there was the snoring. She pushed the door but found that it had been secured from the inside. She knocked and waited.

'Who is it?' a voice called from the inside.

'It's me,' answered Martha.

'Boela ko tsoang – go back to where you have been,' growled her father. 'I have no house for prostitutes!'

The whole house seemed to be awake now. A din of malicious voices sounded in her ears. George had already left. Even if he had waited outside, he could not have helped her, for he had no room of his own. He lived with his parents and probably slept in the same room. Could his parents also have refused to open for him? No, Martha argued to herself. They would want some of George's earnings.

She knocked again. The door opened abruptly. Her father hauled her roughly into the room and kicked the door closed with a bang that aroused the neighbours.

'Rubbish! rubbish! rubbish! Where have you been for two days?'

Without waiting for an answer he rained lashes on her buttocks.

'Leave my child alone!' shouted her mother.

She pushed herself in between them and demanded to be thrashed herself instead of the child. She knocked on the false wall separating their room from the neighbours' and screamed that by continuing to sleep they wished to see her daughter killed.

Mapena, an old man, well advanced in his years and respected by Mabongo, stepped inside and lighted a candle.

'Mabongo, Mabongo!' called the old man.

9

'Ntate,' answered Mabongo meekly.

'Stop beating her. We shall talk tomorrow.'

While the two men were talking, the old woman, Mapena's wife, pulled the girl by the hand and fixed a bed for her in her room. Martha crept into the blankets and covered her head and sobbed. All was quiet again except for the croaking of throats here and there, like beetles in a graveyard hovering over the silent dead.

Martha dreamt of the funeral of Ma-Ndlovu's husband. The coffin moved slowly from the room and two women, dressed in deep mourning clothes, sobbed bitterly behind the corpse. They uttered words that sounded like the pleading of a rainmaker for the gods to wet the dry land and quench the thirst of the sheep and goats whose faces were turned to the sky. The taller of the women appeared to have collapsed and fainted. The other elegantly stepped into the mourning coach and sat there unconcerned about her partner. A man seemed disgusted, and packed clothes which he threw into a wooden box and then waved farewell to the others.

Martha got up the following morning to make fire in the open brazier as usual. Her limbs were sore and her joints stiff. She shook the ashes from the brazier so as to leave the half-burnt coal and sprayed the remainder with water. Her father, who worked in a dairy and had to leave at three o'clock to be in time for the early deliveries, had already gone.

'Moipone,' called her mother from inside the room, 'It is not going to be long before you are ready to have a child. We are wasting our money sending you to school. You see that your father is not a healthy person. If he dies and you have a child there will be nobody to pay rent and buy food. You really ruin my health, Moipone.'

Mrs Mabongo wept and thought of her parents who had strongly opposed her marriage to Mabongo. She wondered how, if her husband took ill and she became destitute, she would tell her parents. Mabongo's relatives did not recognise her as his wife. If they heard of his illness they would simply remove him without consulting her.

'Ma, Ma,' called Martha, 'what's the matter?'

'You are causing all this anxiety for me. You go about at night. I have a great fear about your night visits.' She paused and remained silent for a considerable time.

'Call your grandmother.'

Martha called the old lady whom she called grandmother and when Mrs Mapena entered, Martha was ordered to remain outside.

'Ausi Ma-Mapena. I want you to undress Moipone and find out if she has slept with boys.'

It was a Monday morning and Martha was preparing to leave for school.

'Don't go to school today,' said her mother.

Martha was ordered inside. Ausi Ma-Mapena examined Martha's body and reported her to have had intercourse several times. In the evening

10

Mrs Mabongo reported the findings to her husband and they decided to stop her attending school.

The day following the incident of her beating, Martha sent a message to George, asking him to meet her that evening at Angle Road, the street behind the one in which she lived.

'George,' she appealed to him, 'I have lost my education through you and I have also had an unpleasant examination. I have told my parents that I have slept with you.'

'Then what did they say?' inquired George.

'They said that you have to be blamed if anything goes wrong with me.'

George said nothing.

'Don't you love me any more, George?' Martha asked.

He inquired why she had asked such a question and Martha told him that she had never seen him so quiet. He had not even kissed her. George smiled and pressed her against him and kissed her.

'Martha, of all the women, I love you the most.'

'But if I get pregnant, you won't want me more than other women.'

George smiled and said she would not fall pregnant.

'Did you get your money from Auntie Ma-Ndlovu?' asked Martha.

'No,' replied George, 'My mother said she would go there soon after the funeral.'

'How is she going to get her to pay? She will make the excuse that she has spent all the money in burying her husband.'

'She has made money from the Marabi Dance and the people have been collecting for a whole week. Vuzi's uncle has bought two sheep, and an ox is to be bought on Friday. How can she spend so much money and forget to pay her debts? Ma will see that I am paid. She can fight!'

'Moipone!' called her mother the next morning, 'you are today a woman. You must behave like a woman. Women do not hang about on the street corners at night. They prepare meals for their men. You must wear long dresses over the knees. Your father has given me money to buy you cloth for dresses and I don't want to see you sitting around the fire outside in the evenings. Women don't sit outside round fires like children. When they are not married, they help their parents by washing clothes or selling beer. A girl who does not behave like a woman never gets married, and if she neglects her duties, she loses her man. My child, men are selfish, they want to be treated like children. They won't help in the house and yet expect the woman to be ready with food any time they are hungry. "I want food!" they demand when they are hungry.'

Martha nodded all the time her mother was speaking. She had heard her father shouting to be given food any time he wanted it.

Later that afternoon, Mrs Mabongo went with Martha to the Vrededorp shops and spent more than five pounds on clothing and on a pair of ladies' shoes.

'Is she getting married, mosali mogolo?' asked the Indian storekeeper.

'No. I want her dressed like a woman so that she can get a man who is wealthy with cattle to pay bogadi.'

'How many cattle do you want for her?' asked the storekeeper.

Mrs Mabongo counted on her ten fingers and raised two more fingers.

'Too much!' said the shopkeeper.

'You are also charging too much for your goods! Why shouldn't I charge what I like for my child? I carried her nine months before birth and suffered pains to bring her to this earth and stayed awake all night when she was not well. Do you think I must give her away magala?'

'But the boy's parents had the same trouble, and he has to work for her and the children,' pursued the shopkeeper.

'A man must buy a wife, otherwise men can just come and take her away,' insisted Mrs Mabongo.

When Martha and her mother left the shop, they carried extra goods, given to them by the storekeeper.

'Tsamayang pila,' he called to them in farewell as they walked down the street.

2

THE FUNERAL BELL rang and rang and rang, and beat sorrowfully into the hearts of hundreds of people who had come to bid a last farewell to Vuzi, the son of Madondo, the husband of Ma-Ndlovu.

'Gong! . . . gong! . . . gong!'

'He who is born of man and woman shall not live for ever on this earth. God so loveth his only son that he gave him to be crucified to save our sins.'

'Gong! . . . gong! . . . gong! . . . gong!'

Reverend Ndlovu was born in Northern Rhodesia and came to the Union of South Africa as a contract labourer to a farm. He was illiterate and had learned to 'read' the bible by memorizing what he had heard. When conducting a service he hid his illiteracy by looking closely into the bible from his place behind the pulpit; and he never made the mistake of 'reading' anything that was not written in the Book. He was greatly helped in his work by listening to street corner services, and by never failing to attend funeral services conducted by others in the hope that he would be called upon to assist.

Thus those who had no minister to go to when there was a death in the family, engaged the services of the Reverend A. B. Ndlovu. In appreciation he was given a couple of pounds by the bereaved persons.

His proper name was Tshirongo. He had changed to the name of Ndlovu when the police organized a swoop on 'Foreign Natives' and sent them home in their thousands. He had married one of the daughters of the foreman on the Bethal farm where he worked his contract of service, and when he was free to leave, had loitered about for a short period, studying the way the services of the Apostolic Faith Church of Zion were conducted. After gaining the confidence of some of the leading members of the church, he led a deputation to the Native Commissioner. Under oath – 'I swear that I am telling the truth' – he was given an exemption pass under the name of Ndlovu. Again under oath, he gave them to understand that he had been ordained a priest by the Right Reverend Mtembu of the whole Bethal District before the witness of three Church Elders.

Reverend Ndlovu walked out of the office of the Native Commissioner in ecstasy, waving the Exemption Certificate in the air, his white teeth in the photograph showing whiter than the paper on which it was printed. That night, the bells in the African quarters rang tumultuously, and a service was held attended by thousands of people. Five sheep and several head of cattle lost their lives that weekend.

The fame of the man spread far beyond the borders of Bethal, and the Prospect Township church circuit requested his services. There he performed ceremonies and attended parties and Marabi Dances, and won many members for his church.

'Gong! . . . gong! . . . gong! . . . gong!'
'He that believeth in God shall not die.'
Reverend Ndlovu did not puzzle his listeners, for he always explained to them that only the flesh dies and the soul ascends to heaven and sitteth on the right hand of the Father.

He was not requested to officiate at this funeral. But he knew that the woman had had Marabi party dances and brandy gatherings of well dressed men, as well as a beer kgotla (or meeting). So he made it his business to assist at the proceedings. In doing this, he thought he might solve his problem of going back to Rhodesia.

'If I win her confidence, my next step is to make love to her, then my way to wealth will be easier. I am going to spend every night at the vigil and preach and preach,' he planned. 'If I get the money, I shall take the first train to Rhodesia. I want to be called Mr Tshirongo. Damn Ndlovu! That is not my proper name.'

He had sent his wife and children to Rhodesia during the mass raids against the 'foreign natives' and now he hoped to make a few more pounds before he joined them.

He was much relieved when Ma-Ndlovu called on him after the funeral

13

to ask him to help her calculate her expenses. She made the invitation on the understanding that he would act as her brother since they bore the same surname.

'Uncle,' Ma-Ndlovu had said to her husband's uncle, 'my brother, Reverend Ndlovu, will take over the responsibility of paying the funeral expenses.'

'Since when has Reverend Ndlovu been your brother?' inquired the old man.

'Hau! Baba mcane, little father, Reverend Ndlovu is my father's younger brother's son, just like you and Vuzi.'

'You should have told me before,' insisted the old man.

'How could I speak to you about my relatives when I had to sit at my husband's head?' said Ma-Ndlovu angrily.

'I undertook to buy two sheep and an ox. Is he going to refund me the money?'

'Umhlolo! You surprise me! How can you expect to be refunded the money you spent on your brother's child?'

'Ma-Ndlovu! Now I know why you demanded the body of Vuzi. Eat your money with your new brother! The spirit of Madonda will haunt you until you go to the grave!'

The old man banged the door, calling her 'Isifebe! Prostitute!' as he left the house.

Soon afterwards, Reverend Ndlovu arrived to help count the money. Ma-Ndlovu cleared a table and the count began. She took out notes from all over her body, her clothes, her pockets, her blouse and headgear, from under the mats upon which she was sitting. Pound notes, moulded with perspiration, some of them disfigured, fell to the floor. Reverend Ndlovu wiped his brow and rushed in excitement to secure the door which he barricaded and locked. Then they began counting and counting and recounting. They argued between themselves and disputed the totals. Ultimately they counted in fives and calculated from the five fingers of the hand, placing the money aside in two groups to represent two hands and finally they arrived at the right figure: forty-five pounds and ten shillings.

'How much have you still to pay for funeral expenses?' asked Reverend Ndlovu.

'It's all paid,' replied Ma-Ndlovu.

She tied the money in an old rag and fastened it to her waist inside her dress. Then she lifted a dilapidated mattress and removed a pile of paper packets in which more pound notes were crammed. As before they counted and recounted: there were a further twenty seven pounds. These she placed in her blouse. Then from a corner of the room she fetched two syrup tins from which she poured the pennies and the silver.

Rap . . . Rap . . . Rap. There was a knock at the door.

'Ma-Ndlovu vula – open!'

'Ngubane?' inquired Ma-Ndlovu.

'Umama uka George. I want the money you owe him.' George's mother began banging the door and kicking it, and when this was not successful, she picked up a brick and threw it through the window, breaking the panels and the glass.

'It is George's mother,' said some of the girls who had been at the Marabi Dance eight days before. A crowd gathered to see what would happen.

'Yooo! Yooo! Let her open the door. Ma-Ndlovu has locked herself inside with the Minister, with Mfundisi!' they screamed.

'Haaaaaa! Her husband was buried yesterday,' roared the mothers and the children.

The window had been completely broken and Ma-Ndlovu and the Reverend hid behind the furniture. George's mother peeped through the window and hurled another brick which caught the Mfundisi on the head and the blood flowed freely onto the floor. Ma-Ndlovu unfastened the door and threw it wide open and flung a full tin of silver coins to George's mother.

'Hamba! We are Christians. We don't want to rob anybody,' she shrieked.

George's mother opened the tin but was not satisfied and threw it back at her. 'I want paper money, I want paper money!' she roared and puffed like a tigress, and rushed inside hauling out the Mfundisi like a twenty five pound bag of mealie meal. The Mfundisi, an active agile man, sprung quickly to his feet and darted back into the room.

'Kahle mama. Wait!' The Reverend Ndlovu was breathless. 'Ma-Ndlovu, give her five pounds.'

Ma-Ndlovu turned to a corner of the room and took out from her blouse the required money and handed it to George's mother. The crowd taunted them.

'You have fixed her right. She has made business from her husband's dead body. We will never attend her Marabi parties any more. *Siiiii*, that Mfundisi sleeps with women during the day. See how the blood drops from his head. It proves that he is a sinner. . . . '

The police arrived and after inquiries dispersed the crowd.

'Mfundisi, I am going to send you to take all this money to the Post Office,' said Ma-Ndlovu. 'When you have finished with that you must go and look for Alberto at the mine compound.'

'Give me a half-jack of brandy first so that I can have no fear against anybody,' the Mfundisi asked.

She handed him a bottle and he drank half of it without stopping. He coughed a bit and then put the bottle down and held his hands on his abdomen.

'Now give me a bottle of chechisa to help the brandy down.'

He drank without stopping, shaking his head all the time as though he were removing the dust from it.

'Now kiss me to drive the evils away.'

She held him by the neck and pushed her tongue through his mouth. He pressed her close towards him and they twisted their tongues together like a cow and its calf.

'Go Umfundisi. The Post Office will close at four o'clock. I don't want the money to sleep in the house.'

The Reverend staggered to the door, supported himself by it, shook his head to come to his senses, and stepped into the street. Before he had left with the money, Ma-Ndlovu had tied it securely around his waist, the pound notes parcelled in five-pound bundles and each bundle tied separately.

'I am drunk now,' he thought. 'I must go to the prophet and get some of his water which will make me vomit. His water is magical. It leaves one without any of the effects of vomiting. I shall be alright very soon.'

'Saaaaakuuuuuubona, prophet,' greeted Reverend Ndlovu, staggering and swaying from side to side. The prophet eyed him closely and bade him be seated. He supported himself by the table and sat clumsily on the bench. Having seated himself, he dropped his head on the table and watered it with saliva.

'Hallelujah! God of Israel, God of Moses, God of Chaka, God of Moshesh, God of Senzangakona, God of Nkukunyana. Kupa satane – take away the devil from this man. He has been bewitched by a woman. A woman who sleeps with evil spirits, with Tokoloshi. Puma satane! Get out, devil! Puma satane!' As he said this, the prophet held his hands on the man's forehead. He lifted his chin and applied very cold water, dabbing some of it on his brow. From a corner of the room he fetched a bowl of black water and had him drink it until his stomach was as taut as a drum. He placed a bowl, spread with green leaves along the bottom, before him, and then uttered a few inaudible sounds.

Suddenly the Reverend bent down and vomited into the bowl. A dreadful stench filled the room. The prophet tightly closed the window which had been half open and drew the tattered curtains in order to prevent the slightest light from penetrating.

'I thank you Ma-Kosi ame. You have taken the Devil out of him.'

The prophet handed Ndlovu a plate of soft sour maheu – porridge – together with a big lump of meat, and ordered him to eat.

'Amadlosi – the spirits – are not thanked, you understand. Go in peace Umfundisi. The Tokoloshi which the woman had bewitched is drowned in this bowl.' He stirred the object that had passed from Ndlovu's stomach into the bowl with a short sharp spear which had been smeared with fat. With the point of the spear, he pierced a large lump in the bottom of the basin and lifted from it a grotesque shaped creature.

'I have killed the Tokoloshi which could have ended your life. Gods of Mzilikazi and Lobengula be with you!'

The Reverend bade the prophet farewell and walked towards the end

16

of the township nearest the mine compound. His stomach still rumbled and his head felt dizzy but clearer.

'I must catch the Mafeking–Rhodesia train tonight without fail,' he said to himself.

Reverend Ndlovu's room faced the main road and a bus running between Johannesburg Station and the City Deep Mine passed in front of his door. He possessed only one suitcase which he packed with clothes and children's religious books, showing the children of Israel in Egypt and Moses on the Mount of Sinai. Another book portrayed a black Moses addressing a multitude of people, and among the crowd, several men dressed in black uniform and some in plain clothes took notes of what the speaker said.

The suitcase was heavy. 'I don't mind throwing out some of the clothes, and this old book of the bearded white man on the mountain, but this of the black man speaking to the people, I must take to Rhodesia and show to my people there.' His thoughts raced ahead. 'When freedom has come, I shall not only be an Mfundisi but a Minister of Religion. I am already a rich man.' He felt his waist. The money was still there. 'I am going to give the people five pounds and I am going to build a house in which the people will be free to hold meetings. The bus is coming. I thank the Gods of Lobengula that Ma-Ndlovu does not yet know that I have not taken the money to the Post Office. I must get out of Johannesburg by tonight, before she finds out that I have not gone to see her Alberto.'

The bus drew up towards the kerb and the Reverend boarded it.

'All fares. Where do you get off?'

'Social Centre,' replied the Reverend.

'Kipa sooka – pay sixpence.'

'I won't take the chance of getting off at Park Station,' the Reverend thought to himself. 'There are too many detectives there.' At the Social Centre he found a ricksha.

'Hey! Ricksha, ricksha. How much to Mayfair?'

'Hlof kron,' replied the feathered runner. He meant 'half a crown.'

'Alright! Laisha!' shouted the Reverend, climbing into the cart.

'Run!' he commanded, lifting his walking stick as if to strike the man. The time was six o'clock in the evening and the Mafeking–Salisbury train left the platform at six thirty.

There was the usual long queue of passengers for the main line trains, and the booking clerk was slow. He fumbled and cursed and smoked and sometimes closed the pigeon hole through which he handed the tickets, in order to finish what he was doing.

'Hoekom het jy nie daardie geld reggemaak nie?' the clerk yelled at a woman in front of the Reverend, 'why didn't you change that money?'

The sweat poured down the Reverend's face. He had a five pound note and only needed a few shillings change. 'If he insists, I shall tell him to keep the change.'

'Epi wena hamba, Mfundisi? Where are you going?'

'Bulawayo.'

'Haikona Bulawayo lapa. Not for Bulawayo here. Mafeking and Salisbury kopela. Next!' screamed the harassed clerk.

'Please baas neka – give me Salisbury then. Keep the change!'

The booking clerk smiled and hurried to issue the ticket.

'Ja, hamba kahle Umfundisi. Go well, minister.'

The time was 6.25 p.m. The vanman was already standing on the platform and was waiting for the last postbag to be loaded. The Reverend came down the steps. 'Kahle baas. Wait!' He dashed onto the platform and got into the last coach. A green flag was waved and the train slowly pulled out of the station.

'Nee, hy is nie in die trein nie,' he heard a plain-clothes man say to one of the African police. Who was not on the train? He trembled.

The Reverend walked to the carriage, as ordered by the guard, and got himself a compartment together with two other passengers heading for Plumtree. The train stopped at Langlaagte and picked up a group of country women and a few men who spoke Sechuana. One among them spoke Zulu. To the Reverend's ears the voice sounded like a woman's he'd heard at Prospect Township.

'Solly brother, me go lavatory. Look after my goods,' he asked a man in his compartment and disappeared until he felt safe. The train sped on, leaving Johannesburg, passing Krugersdorp, Magaliesburg, Zeerust, the bush and thick grass of the Western Transvaal, and at last reaching Mafeking.

Ma-Ndlovu, on failing to see the Reverend or Alberto return, went to the police station nearby and reported that a man had robbed her of the money she had collected for her husband's funeral expenses. Her statement read to the effect that the robber had been dressed as a priest and had got through her window by first breaking the glass with bricks and then had entered the house and forced her to hand him all the money she had collected. She described the robber as tall, lean but healthy, very dark in complexion, with flimsy but coarse hair, unlike most of the local Africans. He spoke Zulu but was not perfect in his speech.

'Did you not scream to attract attention?' asked the officer.

Ma-Ndlovu stuttered 'I . . . I . . . did not scream.'

'Why did you not scream?'

She kept quiet.

'Were the windows not broken by a woman who came to claim money for her son who had played for your Marabi Dance the Sunday your husband was killed by a motor car?'

Ma-Ndlovu asked him how he knew all this. The Officer explained that it was he who had inquired into the disturbance and ordered the crowd to disperse.

'Did you not give the money to Reverend Ndlovu? Perhaps you trusted him to take it to a place of safety?' asked the Officer.

'I . . . I . . . gave it to him to take to the Post Office and he hasn't returned.'

'Alright, Mrs Alberto, I shall help you to get the man arrested if we can find him.'

All the police in the area were given the description of the Reverend who was well known to them. They combed the township and the mine compound. They extended their search to the new township, Orlando, but nobody knew such a priest nor had they ever heard of him. A clue was found from the bus conductor who said that a priest answering the description had caught the bus on Monday at 4.30 p.m. and had alighted at the Bantu Men's Social Centre.

The police hurried to the spot and made further inquiries from the Wemmer Barracks Police. 'No such man seen here,' replied the insolent African policeman. 'They think our job is to know the face of everyone who enters this gate.'

A ricksha-puller, who happened to be nearby overheard the conversation. 'Yini?' The policeman told him that they were looking for a man dressed as a priest who had cheated a woman of her money on the previous afternoon. The ricksha-puller told them that he had taken such a man to the Mayfair Station.

They raced to the Mayfair Station. It was 3.30 p.m. and the same booking clerk was on duty. The clerk was astonished at being expected to remember the passengers who had bought tickets the day before. He looked blank and shrugged his shoulders. 'I serve hundreds and hundreds of passengers daily. I would not even know if I had served my own mother. Hoe kan ek honderde naturelle onthou? How can I remember hundreds of natives?'

They gave up inquiries, deducing that the culprit had left by bus and changed transport on the way in order to throw the police off his trail. He had probably boarded a main line train to Lichtenburg or Mafeking. Or maybe he had taken one of the local trains to Pimville, Kliptown, Lenz or the newly built township at Orlando. Messages with his description were dispatched immediately to these suspected areas and the police combed them for the wanted man.

Mr A. B. Tshirongo emerged from the lavatory no more the Reverend Ndlovu, having discarded his assumed nationality. He was one of the Kalanga, born and bred in British territory. He wrapped his stiff collar in a piece of brown paper and returned to his compartment. He took his seat quietly without showing any sign of emotion and was very reserved when asked about his journey or the place from which he had come.

'I am very tired,' he said, when one of the passengers attempted to start up a conversation.

Before the train reached Krugersdorp he climbed into the top bunk, together with his luggage, and pretended to be snoring. All the time, he kept a sharp ear to catch any suspicious conversation. When the train stopped at a station he preferred to remain on his bunk rather than take the risk of looking outside.

'Mfundisi!' called out one of the passengers.

The Reverend turned angrily towards the speaker, 'I don't want to be awakened when I am asleep. Don't bother me any more with your childish wish to look at people on the station!'

He fell back into a feigned sleep and in two minutes was snoring. The other passengers, having sat until the train had passed many stations, took their places of sleep and slept.

'All tickets. We are now coming in to Koster.' An elderly ticket examiner entered the compartment. Mr Tshirongo did not stir.

'ALL TICKETS!' shouted the ticket examiner.

The Reverend awoke with such terror that he knocked his head against the luggage rack and would have landed on the floor if the inspector had not moved close and prevented him from falling.

'Are you dreaming? Don't you know that you are not sleeping in your house!'

The former Reverend wiped the sweat from his black shining face and grinned, his teeth as white as unstained paper. He hurriedly searched for his ticket and handed it to the examiner.

The train reached Mafeking at 9.00 a.m. As the train steamed into the station, Mr Tshirongo for the first time peeped through the window. There were not many people to receive the passengers. The white people that were there waited at the far end of the platform and none of them showed any interest in the non-white passengers whose coaches were close to the engine.

'She will never see me any more. I am safe now. The distance is too great for the mafukisi to travel.'

After alighting, he took his luggage to the parcel office and had it labelled 'Salisbury'. Having done this, he strolled around the station and bought a tin of coffee from a moving cart and then proceeded to follow the other passengers across the bridge.

'Taxi gentlemen. Two shillings only.'

The taximan opened the door for him and he got in. When the car was full they drove a distance out of town. After the other passengers had alighted Mr Tshirongo got down and paid his fare.

'Thank you,' bowed the taximan.

'Where can I get something to drink?'

'Do you want Kgabi? It's strong drink. Alright, I will take you to my auntie's place.'

They walked a few yards from the taxi rank and went into a house full of men and women drinking.

'Ho gentlemen, here comes Billy with a stranger. A toast to his friend.'

They all stood around the two men and brought out bottles of cane spirits,

'Welcome, stranger, to Mafeking. Lehatse la Bochwana – the land of the Bechuanas.'

'Die een is myne! This one is mine. Come darling. Don't be afraid. Billy is my brother and that one is my brother.'

Mr Tshirongo took a seat between the two young women and was immediately offered a drink. He swallowed the contents in one short gulp and looked at the bottom of the measure to see that he had drunk it all.

'Ish velly nishe. Can you get me another measure?'

They got him a bottle. He drank half before resting for breath and passed the remainder to Billy. He ordered another bottle and more bottles came from all sides.

Luma lumang Barolong. Galo lume galo nkgatle.
Galo etse dinku di lela. Dilela dikunyana.
Luma lumang Barolong. Galo dume galo nkgatle.

Luma lumang Barolong. Galo lume galo nkgatle.
Mosali gase maago, leka metso a kagachoma.
Me ntsoare kea robega. Gake robege ke mabela.'

They sang the song with emotion, and Rebecca who had put her arms around the visitor, found herself kissing him.

'I am going with you to Rhodesia.'

'Me got no money to pay for you.'

'Ag! Darling, you can sleep here tonight. My mother has got a separate room for me. You and I can spend a good night in it.' She spoke softly into his ears.

'Me velly sorry. My suitcase is luggaged and it will leave by tonight's train. I must leave by tonight.'

The girl's hands moved from one of his pockets to the next as she was talking to him, and when he pushed them away she kissed him.

'Don't worry honey. These boys will not hurt you. Billy is their chief.'

'I must leave,' he said, 'my train will pull off before seven o'clock and I must get to the station before it is dark.'

He shook hands with everyone except two men who had been seated apart in a corner of the house, their faces obscured by an open kitchen door.

These men, who had sat silently among the drinkers, sipping their drinks slowly, walked out. One of them followed Tshirongo and the other ran as fast as he could to cut him off from the front. On seeing him approaching a few yards away, he selected a conspicuous shop corner and took out three playing cards and began talking loudly to attract those who passed.

'The red card is the winning card and the two blacks the losing ones. Fanna – fanna. You put two pounds and I give four pounds.'

He shuffled the cards hard against the ground and shifted each card from position to position, his hands crossing one another without rising from

21

the ground. He stood up and looked from side to side, arms akimbo. Mr Tshirongo glanced in his direction.

'Come and try your luck, brother.' He lifted the cards from the ground and began shuffling them again with alacrity. The man who had followed came closer and pointed to a card.

'Show me first your money before I open the card.'

The man produced a wad of pound notes and placed one of them upon the card.

'I win!' announced the player, pretending to be surprised.

'Fanna – fanna. The red card is the winning card and the two blacks the losing ones,' repeated the other.

'Show me, brother?' asked Tshirongo, curious.

The player urged him to point out his card.

Mr Tshirongo pointed toward a card and the gambler lifted it. It was the red one. 'Here's a pound for you. Take it.'

He hesitated. 'Take it,' rejoined the others. 'Don't be afraid, you have won.'

Mr Tshirongo took the pound. The game was repeated a second time, the card player speaking faster and faster, shuffling the cards angrily and waving his hands along the ground.

'Ara-rah! Ara-rah! Police!' People ran in all directions, the police whistles ringing behind them. Mr Tshirongo gazed on, astounded. Just as he was about to move, a policeman took hold of him from behind.

'Come. I am arresting you!'

'Me no play cards. Me pass to Rhodesia. Please policeman.'

Tshirongo and the two other men who had been drinking together were led a few yards from where the gambling game had taken place. They were pushed into a dirty passage, littered with rags and dead cats.

'Search them, Corporal,' commanded one of the men.

The 'Corporal' plunged first into the pockets of one of the two men and removed several pounds. When he had completed the 'search' of the other man, he turned to Tshirongo.

'Morena please! Me no play card. Me go to Rhodesia.'

'Search him. Don't waste time.'

Tshirongo was shaking from top to toe. The 'Corporal' delved into his pockets, and finding nothing there, looked at him suspiciously. He was swaying from side to side like a stalk of maize in the wind.

'Pull off your shoes,' commanded the 'Corporal'. He found nothing.

'Loosen your trousers.'

Tshirongo uttered pitiful pleas and held his trousers fast after loosening his belt.

'You swine. I told you. The Kiriman's got money.' They wrenched the dirty cloth from his waist and without looking at it, the 'Corporal' passed it to the 'Sergeant'.

'Where do you get all this money from? You hond.' Before Tshirongo could answer, his two fellow 'prisoners' joined the Corporal and the Sergeant in kicking him and calling him 'dirty Kiriman'. They chased him along the passages, one of the 'prisoners' brandishing a long knife and following close at his heels. When he came out of the passage into the light he looked about him, dazed. His assailants were nowhere to be seen.

'Hallo, hallo friend,' called a man who happened to be Billy. 'Why do you look so worried?'

Tshirongo could hardly utter a word, until the man came closer to him. 'What's wrong?'

'Two policemen and blue-nines robbed and assaulted me.'

'Ah! I am sorry. You should have waited for me in the house and I would have taken you back to the station. Have you got any money to pay for a taxi ride to the station?'

'They robbed me of all the money I had.'

'How much was it?'

'Lot of money. Me no count.' He raised all his ten fingers twice and showed the other five fingers.

'Lot of money,' said Billy. 'They are not police. They are all blue-nines. All right friend, I will take you for nothing to the station.'

When they had reached the station, Billy gave him a pound note and said he was very sorry and that he would give him more money if he had it. With these words he left, leaving Tshirongo to make his way to the parcel office.

'This Billy must be one of the blue-nines who robbed me. How did he know where I would be at that time? And why does he feel sorry for me? The location children are all crooks. They learn these things in the bio-scopes. I have been a priest and respected by people. The Native Commissioner of Bethal gave me a certificate of priesthood and the people killed two oxen when I was ordained as the Reverend Ndlovu. I have now been touched by profane hands. I have buried the dead and had their sins forgiven, but those blue-nines! I pray for them to go to hell. I didn't steal the money from Ma-Ndlovu. She gave it to me because the gods of Lobengula willed it. And she, Ma-Ndlovu, did not work for it. She staged Marabis and sold beer on Sunday. It's a sin to work on Sunday.

'The police might now be looking for me here. I don't care if they are here. They can take me back to Johannesburg. I haven't got the money anymore. I will tell them that I have been kidnapped and then robbed!' He flung his arms violently and missed a porter narrowly.

'Is jy mal? Are you mad?'

'I am sorry, sir. I have been robbed by blue-nines. All my money is gone.'

The porter stopped and asked him where he was robbed.

'Location.'

'Go and report to the police.'

'To the police? Police no good. Two policemen and two blue-nines kicked me and took my money. How can I go to the police again?'

'I don't think they were police,' said the porter. 'Blue-nines rob people by saying they are the police. Next time you must watch out when people say they are the police.'

'How can I? Police every day ask people for their passes, and if you say you want to see their passes they arrest you and tell the Magistrate you are cheeky. The Magistrate also believes them and he sentences one to jail.'

'You can explain to him that you didn't believe they were police.'

'Ah! my friend, nice because you are a white man. White people believe other white people even when they tell lies and swear to God that they are telling the truth.'

'How do you know?'

'How do I know? Bishop Mtembu was sent to jail for breaking his service contract with a white farmer, because when he wanted to plough according to the agreement, the farmer refused and the Bishop left the farm without notice. The farmer reported him to the police and charged him with desertion and breaking his contract. He tried to explain to the Magistrate that the farmer had agreed to give him four acres for himself to plough and when he wanted to plough according to the agreement, the farmer refused. So the Bishop was arrested and charged and sent to jail. You see, my friend, you are white and I am wrong.'

The porter said he was very sorry about what had happened but thought that what he said about the white people were things he had heard from agitators in Johannesburg. 'You must not believe what these agitators tell you. They only want to get you into trouble. The white man is doing all he can for the black man. You must be good to the baas and the baas will do all he can for you. You hear, my boy?'

Reverend Ndlovu – Mr Tshirongo looked at the man from head to foot. 'Please don't call me "your boy". I am older than you by ten years. Please don't call any man older than you "boy". It's not manners.'

'Take, here's a shilling,' ventured the porter.

'Keep your shilling! I shall not take a shilling from anybody who has no respect for me. Goodbye.'

He walked away, no longer thinking about the robbery but about the porter calling him 'boy'. 'Good Heavens! White people have no respect for a black man. I am glad I have not lost my luggage. I shall show my people the black Moses speaking to his people about freedom and then they can tell the white men who call them "boys" to stop it.'

The guard waved the green flag and the train puffed out of the station. Mr Tshirongo, dismayed by the robbery and the insult of the porter, took his seat quietly among the other passengers and contemplated his plans. He covered his face with his hands and murmured inaudible words. His thoughts flashed back to Prospect Township.

'This train has run a night, it is too far from the place I come from.' He pictured his wife and children welcoming him, the kids searching his pockets for sweets and him carrying the suitcase into the hut.

'Oh Nkosi yeme! Life is a mist in the morning which breaks off and leaves the hot sun to scorch the grass so that the animals starve.' He leaned against the window and shamelessly shed tears. 'Bantwana bame, bantwane bame – my children, my children, your father has come home poor and destitute.'

Africans are more pleased to welcome a relative who has long been away than one who often visits home. They believe that it is his ancestors who bring him home. Cattle and goats are slaughtered to thank the gods. Dead brothers' wives rejoice that the young father of their future children has come – that now they shall beget more children and add to the family.

Tshirongo was welcomed home by the beating of drums to inform the village that a man 'long left home' had come back. All his wives prepared reed mats for the 'small father' to rest on. Led by the elder wife, his own wife, they walked on their knees and hands with their faces turned downwards: 'Mulungu afika – God has come. God has come.'

3

THREE MONTHS HAD passed since Martha had left school. She received a letter from her teacher saying that he would be calling to see her parents.

Dear Martha,

I am coming to your home on Friday to speak to your parents about your leaving school.

The pupils are missing you very much, and without you and Tom, who has also left school, the choir is very poor. I am sorry that you did not remain to complete your Standard Five. The class has taken a test in preparation for the final examination in December.

Best regards to your father and mother.

Yours sincerely,
S. Lomane.

The letter was given to Tiny, who was now in Sub B.

'Ausi Moipone, here is a letter for you,' said Tiny entering the yard from Staib Street. Martha heaved a sigh and asked who had written to her. 'Your teacher,' said Tiny.

'Moipone! You have started again to receive letters from boys. You will never be a woman. I am going to tell your father.' Her mother rushed out of the door and snatched the letter from her hand and unsealed it. She scanned the lines and called another girl of Martha's age to read it for her.

'Auntie, it's from teacher Lomane, Martha's class teacher. He says that he will be coming on Friday to talk to you and Uncle about Martha having left school.'

The woman smiled. 'Perhaps he would like to marry her.' She counted her ten fingers. 'I shall tell him to pay magadi immediately. I hate the business of men saying they first want children before they marry. Moipone!'

'Ma.'

'Here is a letter from your teacher. He says he is coming on Friday to talk to me and your father. What is he going to say? Did you promise to marry him? Teachers, teachers! They never marry. They just spoil one's child and then go and marry nurses. I shall put hot water on him if he comes here.'

'Ma,' interjected Martha, 'Don't talk like that. Teachers are respectable people.'

Mr Lomane arrived on the Friday afternoon dressed in his best suit. He walked hesitantly into the yard.

'Hallo, children. Where's Martha's mother's home?'

'There, teacher,' answered a group of children playing in the yard and running over the younger ones who lay on the ground pretending to be asleep.

Tiny, who had seen the teacher a few yards away from their home, ran to tell Martha that he was coming. Martha wore a dress that came well over her knees, and a heavily starched apron protecting her dress. She looked more her mother's age than a girl of sixteen years. Her full-throated voice vibrated like a drum-beat as she told her mother that the teacher was being brought in by the children.

'Lumela Ma – goodday mother.'

'Ahe ngwana oa ka – goodday, my child. Take a seat.'

There was one chair which had been upholstered and this was made ready for the teacher to sit on. He wiped his brow with a white handkerchief, then took out a cigarette and lit it.

'Is this Martha's home?'

'Yes, my child.'

'I have come to speak to you about allowing Martha to take lessons in singing. She has a very beautiful voice and from that she can make a living.'

Mrs Mabongo looked blank and stupefied.

'How can one make a living from singing?'

'I can get a clever man to teach her how to sing better.'

'How can he make her voice different from what it is?'

The teacher thought hard to find words which she would understand. 'You see, mother.' He paused. 'We teachers teach children to say words in any other people's languages and to say them like those people. It is hard to learn, but eventually one can do it. In singing we teach them to sing in tune with the piano and to make their voices sound like a bird's

26

voice, and even better. When they can do that, they can sing to a crowd of people who will pay money to hear them singing.'

'Oh! kea bona nwana oa ka – I see my child. But I haven't got money to pay for her.'

'I have a friend who will teach her for nothing. He knows how well Martha can sing. He has been wanting to train her, and stage concerts for Europeans at a big hall in town.'

'What time is she to take her lessons?' asked Martha's mother.

The teacher started. 'In the evening.'

'Sh! Another trouble for her father to wait all night long for her to knock at the door.'

'Mr Samson is a married man and has been a teacher for a long time. He knows that young girls like Martha need proper guardians. He will definitely never let her come home alone. But I am sorry if the old man has to open the door for her.'

At this point Martha intervened, 'Ma, you got me out of school. Now you want to make it impossible for me to learn anything!'

'Thula! Be quiet!' shouted her mother.

'I won't keep quiet to see myself turned into a country girl who is forced to leave school early and work in the white people's kitchens!'

After the teacher had left, Mrs Mabongo told Martha that she would talk the matter over with her father. That evening they discussed the proposition, and it was agreed that Martha should be allowed to take the singing lessons.

Martha took her lessons with Mr Samson seriously. She had changed over the last few months. She detested the way the girls about her shouted their greetings and spoke loudly to one another.

'I wish I could keep George from his Marabi company, and stop him from riding that shiny, decorated bicycle,' she thought to herself one afternoon when he came riding by, pitched high on the saddle, clutching the ornamented handlebars, with ting-tong bells. He wore white flannel trousers with two flat pockets at the back. The turn-ups measured twenty-four inches in width. He swayed from side to side on the bicycle, blew the hooter and simultaneously rang the bells on the handlebars.

'Hallo Martha!'

'Hallo George! Did you get your pay from Ma-Ndlovu?'

'Yes. My mother went with a chopper and sticks to Prospect Township. Ma-Ndlovu was there counting the money from the funeral. She refused to open the door when my mother knocked and when she did not answer, my mother threw a brick at the window.'

'Hau! George, your mother is very brave. Did she get the money?'

'She got five pounds.'

'Much more than you would have received.'

'I understand that the Mfundisi has absconded with the money. An auntie who is working in Mayfair says she boarded a train with him to Mafeking a day after the burial. She alighted at Zwartruggens and before she left the train she saw the Mfundisi fling his collar through the window.'

'What has happened to Ma-Ndlovu?' asked Martha.

'Ah! You women are inquisitive.'

'George, you call me a woman.'

'Yes I do, because you are dressed like an old auntie. Long German print dress, headgear fastened like a makoti.'

Martha looked down shyly and made figures in the sand with her feet.

'I have heard,' continued George, 'that your parents would like you to be married to a country boy.'

Martha gave him a vague smile and looked him straight in the face 'I don't care who marries me. I want a man who will take care of me and make a home for my children.'

George perspired and wiped the sweat from his forehead. His heart burned with jealousy against a man he did not know. 'I will kill him if I see him,' he thought to himself.

Mr Samson was proud of Martha's progress. 'I have asked Miss Treswell to rehearse you for two weeks before the night of Mr Petersen's party. Mr Petersen has come from America.'

Martha worked hard at the rehearsals and was away from home much later than usual.

'Moipone!'

'Ma.'

'You have started again coming late. You shall never be a woman. Your children will fall into the fire. Ah! A woman who goes about at night fights with her husband every night.'

'I don't want a country man to marry me,' answered Martha.

'Mehlolo! Do you think I have given birth to you for nothing? If you don't listen to what your father and mother tell you, you must get out of our house.' Mrs Mabongo bent low down towards the floor, clutched the grass broom and swept the floor as vigorously as she could, spitting where Martha had been standing. 'Siss bana ba kajeno – children of today! They don't listen to their parents. Moipone!'

'Ma.'

'Don't stand there like a woman. Why don't you get food ready for your father. I wish God had denied me children. Women who have no children are better off.'

Mr Ndala and Martha's father were cousins, for Ndala's mother was an elder sister of Mabongo's father. The two cousins had grown up together in her house. They herded the cattle together and went to the circumcision school in the same year. Masekosana, Mabongo's aunt, held both boys in high esteem, and when they went to the circumcision school she undertook the engagement of a private doctor to 'incise' the boys with strong medicines against witchcraft. The doctor arrived at her home in the middle of the night, when the boys were under the strict supervision of the circumcision superintendent and his chief doctor. The old lady bribed them to allow the boys to return to her home for a few hours to receive Mabongo's traditional clan instructions on how to withstand the 'incision of manhood'.

The boys were led into a dark hut. Masekosana and the doctor undressed them, leaving only a strip of skin-cloth around their loins. The two adults then sang mournful songs calling upon the spirits of the dead: 'Woza nina Mabongos – come all Mabongos. Let not your spirits desert the two boys. Let no medicine pollute their food.'

The boys were then 'incised' between the toes and fingers and on the elbows, carotid, back of the neck and on the forehead. When this had been done a black, burning substance was rubbed into the cuts. They were then made to eat raw meat which had been mixed with a red, powdered salve. Not a word was spoken during the ceremony. When all had been completed the boys were returned to their guardians.

'You are going to marry Sarai, my youngest daughter,' said Masekosana to her nephew when he returned from the initiation school. He was thirteen, but it was customary for betrothals to be arranged for very young couples, even children.

He went to work as a farm labourer and gave his first earnings to his aunt with instructions that part of it was to buy dresses for Sarai – 'my young wife'. But he did not marry Sarai. Anger and frustration struck brother and sister when they heard years later that July, as Mabongo was called in the city, had taken a woman far away in the town and that they had had a child.

'He has defied the gods of the Mabongos and he shall be rewarded for it!' Mabongo's father, a much feared witch doctor, assured his sister Masekosana. 'My father would have ended his life if he had dared defy his orders.'

'I have loved my nephew as much as my own son and wished him to inherit part of my wealth, cattle, goats and my art in medicines,' said Masekosana. 'He has not only disappointed you, and the gods of our forefathers, but the whole tribe of the Ndebeles. Our father was a respected man. You are feared by Chief Thulare, the great Chief of the Bapedis. They dare never refuse you a woman. But your own son has defied you. If you are my own father's and mother's child you will not allow him to enter your kraal.'

'He will not enter my kraal while I am still alive,' the eldest Mabongo swore by the gods of Mathathakanye, the great-great grandfather of his father.

The two cousins did not see each other for twenty-three years. Then one day they met in a street of Johannesburg city. They embraced and sat on the pavement and looked at each other, as if July was looking at Sarai, and she at him.

'Where is Sarai?' was his first question.

'Married in Thaba Tsoe, many, many years ago.'

Ndala told his cousin that he had a son who was already working in the suburbs of the city. He had often hoped that he would marry a relative.

'I have a daughter, old enough to be married. If we could unite the two children, it would be a good thing to bring blood of the same blood together.'

'It would also help to reconcile your father and my mother to you.'

The two men bade each other farewell and arranged to meet again and promote the match between their children.

'I have met my cousin, Ndala, and he would like to come and see us,' Mabongo told his wife when he reached home after work.

'Today your people are ready to forgive you because you have a daughter who is old enough to be married. Ah! They think they can save bogadi. Never! You have not paid even a fowl for me. Who are they to claim my daughter's bogadi?'

'My cousin is not coming to claim Moipone's bogadi. He is interested in his son marrying Martha and I also want them to marry. He has a lot of cattle and goats. All I would have inherited from his mother, has been given to his son. The boy does not even need his father to help him pay bogadi. They would return all that I would have got, in the form of bogadi. Over twenty cattle and forty goats. You are a foolish woman! You don't listen first before you speak, and if you speak like this when my cousin or his son is here, we are certain to fail to arrange the marriage of Moipone and my cousin's son.'

'Hau! Ntate Moipone! Father of Moipone! I did not say he would claim the bogadi.' She paused and looked appealingly towards her husband's face. 'I shall tell Moipone to put on her mochikisa. She shall look like a woman! Modisane! Your cousin will never let his son disappoint him!' She began singing: 'Modimo ona le mogau – God has mercy.' She walked out of the room and returned with a scale of beer and went down on her knees to hand it to her husband.

The day had been extremely hot, and when the evening came, its breeze was a blessing. The sky, without stars in sight, predicted rain.

'In the old days, men, women and children would go out amongst the graves and make supplication before the dead who lay buried there. After much praying and dancing and offerings, tjwala would be poured upon the burial place of the grandmothers and grandfathers. Then the supplicants would return to their homes without looking back from whence they had come. A heavy rain would follow and the maidens would dance for joy in the rain.' So spoke the old man who lived in the same yard as the Mabongo family. He went outside, looked up at the sky and came in and told them that it was certain to rain that night.

The Indian shopkeeper, having retired to the back room without closing the shop, joined his aged father and wife, who despite the heat sat around the open brazier fire. The old man held two small drums between his feet and when his son had joined them, began pummelling them mournfully, as if calling upon the dead to rise. His son and wife accompanied the beating of the drums by singing a melancholy song. A baby who had been laid down on the floor turned its eyes from grandfather to father and looked up at the ceiling, as if receiving from Allah an answer to his parents' pleas. The grandfather responded to the baby's gurgling by beating the drums solemnly.

In their part of the cottage, the Mabongos ate in silence. When the evening meal was over, Tiny and the others went out to play hide and seek, or Black Maipatile as they called it. Tiny almost bumped into Martha as the little girl fled through the door of the Indian's shop.

'Bhara – Bhara – blenchud!' screamed the Indian.

'Sorry Ausi Moipone,' spluttered Tiny.

'I have caught you,' claimed a little girl who had been calling 'Black Maipatile'.

'You are cheating!' protested Tiny. 'I was chased by Bhana out of the shop.'

Martha moved aside and gazed into the sky.

Some distance away from the Molefe yard, men pulling rickshas pounded the ground with their bare feet, the dust rising high into the sky. The leader threw himself flat on the ground, turned his face upwards and pointed an assegai to the skies. 'Siyafa makosi – we are dying, chiefs. Siyafa Senzengakona, Siyafa Chaka, son of Senzengakona. Come ye long sought. Ye wombs with dew for my feet to tread.'

At nine o'clock, the sky became pitch black and the air felt damp and clammy. No thunder. No lightning. The sky remained as thick and pregnant as the Maluti Mountains. Then, suddenly, like a dam bursting, water poured from the heavens. The streets were flooded. The yards looked like dams and the water seeped into the houses. The men came out with shovels and opened furrows for the water to pass into the street.

'Balimo ba koathile – the gods are angry,' the old man said.

It rained and rained for a full two hours and then stopped. The sky cleared and but for the frogs, which croaked from far and near, and the puddles of water upon the ground, one would not have known that it had rained. But the Molefe yard was flooded.

'The gods have answered our prayers and now we are engulfed in this yard,' said the old man to his wife. He called Tiny to sleep with them on their bed.

'Come, my grandchild. You will get drowned on the floor.'

The old man called through the thin wooden wall for Martha to come and sleep in their bed too, for the Mabongos' room had been covered by water. 'We don't mind sleeping with them. We are old,' cried the old man.

They all settled in the one room and before long fell into an untroubled sleep.

Martha's father, guided by the carbide light of his cycle, splashed through the yard and waded his way ankle-deep through the pool of muddy water. It took him all his strength to pull his feet and boots out of the slush. One of the lavatories had overflowed and the excrement and urine mixed freely with the mud and water. The stench polluted the air which had been purified by the rain. A tin of skokiaan which had been dug into the ground, to conceal it from the police, lay uncovered and threw a yellow circle of colour, and the whole yard smelled of bread and yeast.

Mabongo stumbled further until he reached the gate.

'Morena! If this is how we live, then God, suffer us all to die.'

He jumped on to the saddle and slowly rode on, his boots full of mud and water as if he had been travelling by night through the countryside. His ankles and knees ached. He sighed and breathed heavily, 'I shall be sixty, twenty years ahead of my age.'

A few hours later the women gathered in the yard. It was a Friday and the women had to brew beer for their week-end customers as early as possible, before the police came on their raids.

'The rain is a nuisance. It makes it difficult for one to brew properly.'

'Why do you waste your time making home beer? You can brew chechisa or skonfana. You know that it gives a stronger kick!'

'Mabongo is having a visitor on Sunday to talk to him about his son marrying Moipone.'

'If you give him the home brew, he won't get drunk quickly and will be shy to say how many cattle he will pay for bogadi.'

'Then I shall take your advice and brew chechisa.'

The women worked steadily at their brew and prepared for the additional visitors they were to receive over the week-end.

On Sundays, scores of people, mostly from the suburbs, flocked to Doornfontein and congregated on the pavements in groups. They greeted each other loudly and laughed with their mouths as wide open as they could get them. The men shook hands with each other, and on seeing a woman they knew, rushed at her and kissed her as if they would swallow her. They dressed in their best clothes: navy blue suits, leopard-coloured lumber jackets, bright red shirts, and judged as the best dressed those who wore fish-tailed coats, waistcoats, a white pocket handkerchief and extra ones in the sleeves. To complete the outfit they wore pairs of small or outsize spectacles and bore expensive walking sticks to add a finish to their appearance.

The women were usually conservatively dressed. Well-tied headgear, a skirt, an umbrella, whether fine or fair, and a pair of flat shoes, made a woman well-dressed and offered good promise of her being chosen as a wife.

The men who dressed themselves for Sunday did not wish to return to the suburbs without having seen one of their 'sisters', who might luckily have found a 'brother' to hire a room for her in one of the yards, where she would rear his children; the offspring assuming their mother's surname because 'you have not paid bogadi.'

Scores and scores of people trudged in the mud. In almost every house there was a beer party. Benches and chairs creaked. The smoke from pipe tobacco and cigarettes rose as high as the rafters and gave out a stifling smell that made Martha cough like a T.B. sufferer.

'Hii, Moipone, come near me. I want to marry you.' A drunken man pulled her by the skirt and patted her on the buttocks.

'Siss, leave me!' She wrenched her body from his grip.

'All right, go and call your mother. Ausi, I want to speak to you.'

'Speak here!'

'No, it's private.'

'Sooka! You propose to my daughter and now you also want to propose to me. I shall tell Moipone's father.'

They drank and drank and drank. In case the police should come, they drank the beer without taking the measure from their mouths and held on to their stomachs as though they were in pain.

It was on this Sunday in the summer, a day after the heavy rain, when the Malaitas and the men and their 'sisters' had congregated near No. 26 Staib Street, Doornfontein, that Mabongo's cousin Ndala, called to discuss the marriage of Moipone and bring together the blood of Mabongo and Mathathakanye.

Ndala bore himself haughtily, swinging his walking stick from side to side and bowing greetings to the attractively attired 'sisters'. He was escorted by two gentlemen who swung their walking sticks in the same manner.

'Ausi Moipone, the people who are going to marry you are coming! They are speaking to that mother.' Tiny nudged Martha by the arm and giggled. 'Siii Ausi Moipone, I am going to be your straw-messie.' A straw-messie is a bridesmaid.

'Voetsek!' Martha pushed the child away from her.

Ndala was a man of medium height, about forty years of age, and he bore the same features as July. There was also a distinct resemblance to Moipone, and the man and the girl might easily have been mistaken for father and daughter. He had a bulky body, small nose and prominent brow. He dressed well: he wore a well-cut navy blue suit, with a golden watch chain strung across his waistcoat, black, sharp pointed shoes and a grey Battersby hat. He had cultivated this English style of dress because he worked for a smart men's shop in town, and it was traditional for Arkson and Son to give their employees a good suit every five years of their service. He wore his suits rarely; only when he visited his friends or attended a public meeting in the Market Square, or on the City Hall steps on Sunday afternoons.

'Lumelang bo ma. Good day, mothers!'

'Ahe tichere. We acknowledge your greeting, teacher!'

The women mistook him for a school teacher because of his sophisticated manner.

'Ntsoarele ma, excuse me,' he addressed a woman standing at the gate, then, in English, 'can you tell me which is Mabongo's place?'

Tiny ran towards Ndala, beating her knees as she went. 'You want Moipone's home? Father Mabongo's daughter? Follow me I will take you to the house.' The child jumped from side to side, like a lamb feeding from its mother.

Martha slipped through the back entrance of the cottage and pretended to play at skipping with a group of children who had been waiting for Tiny to return.

'Ah! Ausi Moipone, you are a woman. You can't play with children! Ausi Moipone, Ausi Moipone!' Tiny pulled her by the hand.

'Grandfather wants you to come and greet the people who are coming to marry you. Come quickly. Yoooooo! Ausi Moipone, the man whom they say is the father of your man is dressed very nice and speaks the white man's language.' Tiny made crude sounds to imitate the white man's language, 'swara-swara and and you hee.'

Martha landed a flat hand on the child's buttocks and Tiny trotted off howling.

Ndala and July greeted each other warmly. Mabongo was surprised to hear that his cousin could pronounce some English words perfectly, and was greatly impressed by a notebook which Ndala produced to write his address in, on a clean white page.

'Hau motsoala, Cousin! You pretend to be an educated man. You with whom I grew up, tended cattle, and went to circumcision school, to lebollo. The white man's school was for the mashaboro. How did you learn to read and write and speak nice English? Tell me, Cousy.'

'The people who speak every Sunday in the Market Square and on the City Hall steps run night schools for us who have grown up,' Ndala replied.

'But,' his cousin persisted, 'it is difficult for a grown person to learn.'

'Some of our teachers are white people and some are black like ourselves, and they have learnt how to teach a grown person. They say we must not worry to learn everything by heart. We mustn't worry to learn all the names of the people who fought in the wars, and who were great men at such and such a time. They teach us how to know why there was a war and who were the people that made them and how wars can be ended.

'And in pronouncing words, they teach us not to read like the teacher whom I heard at home, a b c d e f g h i j . . .'

The women admired him and wished him for a husband.

'I want a man like him to take me to the bioscope.'

'He won't like a woman who walks barefoot!'

Whilst they were talking, a messenger arrived to say that July Mabongo was wanted at the dairy, where he worked. One of the men had fallen ill and July was needed to continue the deliveries. Ndala appreciated the emergency and undertook to wait until his cousin returned. In the meanwhile, he would speak to the women.

The old man who lived in the Molefe Yard was one of the few who understood the laws and customs of the Transvaal tribes, so the tenants of the Molefe yard and a few others in the neighbourhood sought his assistance in matters which needed traditional treatment.

In the matter of Moipone, the old man, who in terms of African custom was regarded as the Mabongos' guardian, came to Ma-Mabongo and said, 'I understand that the man coming here is a cousin to your husband and that they were brought up together, but I am more than that. I have brought up Moipone and have for more than twenty years regarded you and your husband as my children. His close relationship will not prevent me from asking any number of cattle I want for my grandchild, Moipone.' The old man said this in a determined tone of voice and his wife nodded with satisfaction.

The visitors were introduced to the old man by Mrs Mabongo, although she, herself, had not been introduced to them. In the absence of her husband she assumed the position as the head of the house.

'July will probably be late,' she explained to Ndala. 'Your cousin has been working for a dairy since he came to town. I hate dairy work, for one has to work on Sundays as well. The dairy people want to make money on Sundays although the Bible says, "Thou shalt work for six days and rest on the seventh day because the Lord thy God has worked for six days and rested on the seventh day." White people have no respect for what the Bible says. It says "respect thy mother and thy father" and yet they teach their children to call us boys and girls.'

'How can they respect us when their children call the grown-ups by their Christian names?' said Mr Ndala indignantly. 'My employer's child calls her father's sister "Marlene". Aha! I get disgusted when I hear a child call a grown-up person by his Christian name!'

'Cousin,' said Martha's mother, 'we have been living with ntate Mapena for many years.' She spread her whole ten fingers and began counting by placing her fingers on her mouth.

'Many, many years,' commented her cousin, 'and how old is Moipone?' he inquired.

'She was born during the shooting – the general strike in 1922. I was afraid to stay here. My life was saved by my auntie who lives in Nancefield.'

'Many people's lives were saved in Nancefield during lerobo-robo, the influenza, in 1918,' recalled her cousin-in-law, 'because the smell of human waste chased away the sickness. People who lived in town died and we in Nancefield did not die. The masepa (faeces) is a good medicine against lerobo-robo.'

Mrs Mabongo left the room in order to summon Moipone, and the old man addressed himself to Ndala. 'They are your cousins and I say they are my children and Moipone is my granddaughter and it is I and my wife who will have a final say in the marriage.'

'My uncle would be very glad to see that my cousin has gained himself a second father.'

Tiny came leading Martha by the hand.

'Ntate-mohololo,' said Tiny addressing herself to the visitor, 'Grandfather, here's Moipone. She is afraid to come and greet you.' She turned to Martha, 'Yoooo Ausi Moipone. How can you get married when you are afraid of greeting people?'

Martha went down on her knees, cupped her hands and then shook hands with the visitor. She retired to a corner where her grandmother was sitting and went down on her knees, like a lamb, and let her head rest on the old woman's shoulders as though she were pleading for protection.

'I have brought her up from babyhood. She and Tiny are my beloved. They will bury me when I am dead,' said the grandmother.

'I was also brought up by my grandmother, and when I left her to go and look after my father's cattle, she cried like a small child. She used to put away for me whatever food she was given by others, and went without eating for my sake,' recalled cousin Ndala.

At this point, they heard a rattling of tin baths in the corridor. 'Tiny, go and see if it is your uncle in the passage,' ordered the old woman. The child dashed out as fast as a fly and found her 'uncle' chaining his bicycle on to the old baths and discarded pots that were in the passage.

'Now that malumi has come, Ausi Moipone is going to get married,' she said to herself. 'Huuuu, I am going to be a bridesmaid, Grandmother is going to buy me white shoes, a pink dress and a flowery hat.' She picked up a parcel her 'uncle' had left lying on the floor. 'Another grandfather, but not as old as mine, has come and Ausi Moipone was afraid to come and greet him so I pulled her from outside,' she informed Mabongo.

'Why was she afraid?' he asked.

The child giggled and put her tiny fingers on her lips and asked him to bow down. 'Because that grandfather is going to pay cattle for his son to marry her.'

'Who told you that, my niece?'

'Moipone told me and other girls that she was going to be married to a man working in the kitchens and when she saw that grandfather she told us that he was coming to pay, and she said she was no more a girl. She is a woman and is going to be a mother. Uncle, when Moipone has a baby I am going to belega it.' The child moved up and down the passage showing how she would carry Moipone's baby on her back.

Mabongo stretched himself from the cramped position in which he had been riding, smiled at the child and prepared to meet his cousin to discuss the marriage of his daughter, Moipone.

Mabongo's powerful body defied the fatigue and the pains it caused him to feel in his joints. He had pushed his bicycle bravely through a milling and hostile group of Amalaitas. Once, he had been their pinare – as the Ndebele Amalaitas called their champion. He had commanded every single group which came from the areas nearest his home whether they were of his tribe or another. The 'Kings' of other groups had on several occasions challenged him. Mabongo had been fearless and taken them on one by one. When he could not make his opponent withdraw in less than the time he considered long, he would batter with his head and send his opponent whirling around like a dying lion, and thereafter attack everyone within his sight. When all had scattered he would batter his head against every object in his path until Sergeant Van Rooyen of the Marabastad Police Station lifted a hand and ordered him to accompany him to an awaiting pick-up van. The policeman would then deliver him to the Rooiveldt Dairy where he worked.

He had won the love of Mathloare, whom he treated with courtesy and politeness, notwithstanding his violent temper and the coarseness with which he treated his half a dozen other girls. When the Rooiveldt Dairy Company opened another depot in Johannesburg they transferred him there to supervise the 'native boys'. On his Sundays off he visited his old 'home' town, Pretoria, and it was there that he proposed to Martha's mother and suggested that she come to Johannesburg.

'You can already dress like a white missus, and Jo'burg girls dress like that.'

'But you are no good for Johannesburg. Only cheap-line men go to the Amalaita fights.'

'I have stopped!' answered Mabongo, taking an instantaneous decision to place Mathloare before his second love.

He was breathing hard now as he walked along the passage to greet his cousin. His wife came hurriedly towards him.

'Are you sick, ntate Moipone?'

'I am only tired. I shall be alright very soon.'

After washing his face and changing from his overall into a pair of Sunday trousers and a clean shirt, he went to greet his visitors.

'I am pleased you have waited.' He pointed towards Mathloare, 'that is my wife of Marabastad and there is my daughter, Moipone, whom I should like to be married to your son so as to bring the cattle back home.'

He conducted the introductions as formally as though the visitors had just arrived.

'Moipone, have you greeted your father?' he asked. On seeing the frightened look on Moipone's face, he said, 'Come here, moipone. My rakgali, your aunt, will not allow anybody to ill-treat you. She loved me as her own son.'

'Pa, how can I love a man I have never seen? I would like to see him first.' They all laughed, and Tiny ran outside and announced to her playmates that Ausi Moipone was getting married and they began practising wedding songs:

'Ho nyaloa dichabeng go bothloko byang – to be married far away from home is sad.'

'July,' said Ndala earnestly, 'I am very impressed with the manner your daughter has shown us during the few hours we have been here, and I have thought to myself how good it would be if we get my son and your daughter to join each other in wedlock. I am certain my uncle will be very pleased and it would make my mother very happy.'

'Cousy, we cannot guarantee that our children will respect the wishes of their parents. They agree to parents' suggestions and then fail to carry them out. My daughter was born, and has been brought up, in town. She may not well agree with a man born and bred in the country.'

'Ntate Moipone,' interjected his wife. 'Moipone is a woman. She knows how to cook and she dresses like a woman. You want to spoil the marriage for my daughter!'

'My wife, I am speaking of what happens to a girl who has grown up in the town and a young man who has grown up in the country. The town girls want furniture, fancy dresses, nice shoes. They dislike the rough work which is done by country women, and a country man does not understand the life of one who has to buy food, coal, wood, and pay for the roof which he has to keep over his family. He does not understand the life of the town man who has to work for the whole of his life without possessing anything: a house, goats, fowl or cattle. He must always be on the run to go and work. If he loses his work, his children will go without food and be chased out of the house. Moipone must understand that my cousin's son will not like to stay in town. He wants to see his cattle and when he has built up his first home he might like to take another wife.'

'There is only one law for the black man,' intervened the old man. 'If one marries a woman, one marries her for one's parents, and she must go and stay with them until the younger brother marries. The first child belongs to the grandparents and will not live with his parents, and when such a child marries, it is the grandparents who will have the final say. It is wrong for you, July, to say what your daughter will not like. If you like the boy's parents, it is not for your daughter to decide. The boy or girl has no right to refuse the proposals of the parents. The magadi might be paid without the couple even having met each other, and the bride can be taken to the man's parents even if she hasn't seen her man. What you should now say is that your cousin must send other people to have a look at your daughter and these people will return to say how much magadi is wanted. Then women from the man's house will come before the bogadi is paid to satisfy themselves of the looks of the bride. They may refuse the girl if she cannot cook or wash well or keeps the house in dirt.'

During the discussion, Martha and her mother were preparing the evening meal, and after they had all regaled themselves, a four gallon tin of skofana was brought into the room, a young man being given the charge of serving the grown men.

'Ndala,' said Mabongo, 'it has been fortunate that you and I met in the street so that you came today to know my family, and father and mother Mapena. My wife made this beer to entertain you and your friends.'

They drank and the beer sank low to the bottom of the can and their heads buzzed.

'Cousy, you look sick. Your work does not give you time to rest,' said Ndala.

'Yes, I have been working for years on Sundays without a break. My old baas used to give me some Sundays off. He was a very good baas.'

'If he was good, he would have paid wages so that you could go home when you are sick and he should have left money for you before he died. Look, you worked for him when your present baas was still a child.'

'You are right, Cousy. I used to take him to school on my bicycle.'

'Aha! Today he rides in motor cars, one in the morning and another in the afternoon and another for his wife.'

'How do you know that he has many motor cars?'

'Rooiveldt Dairy Company orders suits from our shop. I deliver them to his house. We send cartons of suits for him to choose. Sometimes he takes a dozen at a time and the same number of shoes and shirts, and at the end of the month I fetch the envelope and am told to be careful not to lose it.'

'You have also been working for the same baas for a long time. Why doesn't he give you money to go home?' asked Mabongo.

'You see, he won't give money when others don't. He won't give his workers pensions, as they call it, because the workers have not come together to tell the bosses to pay good wages and to give holidays and to pay us when we take a rest after working for a long time.'

'You are very clever, Cousy. Who told you all about these clever ways? You speak like Makgato of the Congress who walked on the pavement in Pretoria and one day went into a white people's train coach and was arrested. He told the Magistrate that Africa was for the black people and that the white people must go back into the sea. The Magistrate was angry and sent him to prison and old Makgato had hard labour for six months.'

39

'I go to meetings every Sunday in the Market Square and on the City Hall steps. But they don't say we must drive the white people back to the sea. They say we must all live nicely together and be given the same jobs and same pay, like overseas where black people are paid the same money as white people. They say "no colour bar".'

'But Cousy, if they say "no colour bar" and you marry a white woman, who will wash for you because white women can't cook or wash? They just sleep and say, "Annie bring me tea, bring my petticoat and vest", and then they go out into the garden and tell a gardener, "Boy! those flowers are no good, take them out. Go and water those flowers, and when you have finished come and help the girl to wash the dishes".'

'I don't like them too. They are lazy,' answered his cousin. 'But we must not be bad to them. Perhaps when they know we are all people, they will learn to cook and wash for themselves and stop calling us boys and girls.'

The two cousins sat talking until it was dark. The younger men sipped their beer and the women busied themselves in the kitchen going over in detail all that had been said during the course of the afternoon.

A church in Angle Street was holding a concert to raise funds. Martha, already known for her good singing, was to be among the entertainers.

While her father and his guest were drinking and engaged in conversation, she nudged her mother for a talk outside:

'Mother, I have been engaged by the Mvuyane Church to sing this afternoon.'

The Church was only a stone's throw from her home and her mother saw an opportunity to let Ndala hear her daughter sing.

'Get yourself dressed. I will tell your father when you are already there.'

When Mrs. Mabongo and others of the family were not present, Ndala had a chance to ask his cousin how he had come to marry his wife.

'I met her whilst I was working in Pretoria and when I was transferred to this town I went to visit her and persuaded her to come here. She got work in Berea and the following year I had to get a room in Sophiatown for she was pregnant with Moipone. When her parents heard of us living together they were angry and her uncle wanted to come and fetch her, but someone whom I have never seen told them that my father was a feared doctor and he could destroy by lightning in the bright sunshine. So I never saw the uncle who was to fetch her.

'I know that my father and Rakgadi were very angry with me for having failed to marry your sister Sarai, but I couldn't desert a poor girl with a child in her belly.'

'Old people want their own way,' commented his cousin. 'If my son married Moipone my mother would not be able to influence my uncle to chase you away from his home. Moipone looks very much like my sister and my mother will not have the heart to say she is not of her blood.'

Tiny ran into the house: 'Malumi, come and see!'

Mabongo followed her out of the house. When he reached the main gate he saw that some of his old 'home-boys' in the Amalaita game had come to visit him, led by their pinare. They greeted the former Pretoria Amalaita boxing champion with much enthusiasm, prancing and beating their feet on the ground to the time of mouth organ music. It seemed that a big fight had been arranged for this particular Sunday, and though they knew that he had retired from fighting since leaving Pretoria, they now trusted in him to help them keep the championship. Ndala, who had followed Mabongo into the yard, remained silent, but one of the young men who had come with him said, 'We would feel very fortunate if we could see the strength of such a famous pinare as July Mabongo.'

So Mabongo took the mouth organ and led the party of malaitas back to the ring. He played one of the challenging tunes which meant an insult to the other pinares.

Here and there some men went into the ring and exchanged light fisticuffs. July, as he was better known among malaitas, roared and threw up dust with his feet like a bull ready to meet a challenge.

'Prrrrrrr, Petoria ditabeng.'

'Pretoria-Tsoane ea Mamelodi.'

As he called he fisted towards the north. His men waved handkerchiefs over his head and called out 'Arcadia!' and 'Brooklyn!'

The fighting seemed to have got out of order, men were punching each other mercilessly. Then Lektri, the Johannesburg pinare, got into the ring. He was believed to have electric shock punches because of the bangles of copper wire which he wore in abundance and which he got from the Electricity Department where he worked. His pants were divided between the legs by a red patch and lower down, outside the knees, there were patches of cross bones and skulls. Below these signs was embroidered 'Gevaar – danger.' He was a young man and his movements were quick. Before he faced July he displayed his dexterity by hitting the air. Then the two bulls faced each other. It was a fight for July's title as king of Pretoria. The malaitas believed that Pretoria was the most important place because the books of law of the white man were kept there. So the king of the Pretoria malaitas was considered to be the best fighter of all.

For Lektri it was a fight to convince the other groups that the white man's wires on his arms were gevaar.

They hammered each other as bulls of the same strength, beating with heads and fists, kicking and bumping. Bangles on both of them cracked and twisted, blood flowed freely from mouths and noses. Each man used all his strength and cunning to defeat the other.

Lektri found out that the weakness of his opponent was in movement and July found out that Lektri, although fast, was not physically strong enough to stand his grip or a close blow. Like a flashlight Lektri landed fast punches and sent the old champion to the ground. Never had the Amalaita seen Lektri in an acrobatic fight. He displayed his skill while waiting for July to get up. The old bull moved backwards, then charged, landing his head and knees on his opponent's body, holding his head down and battering Lektri's lips and eyes. After a few minutes Lektri fell senseless to the ground.

Mabongo's supporters rushed into the ring and, seizing their hero, raised him onto their shoulders and carried him back to his gate. He and his cousin walked into the house. His wife noticed the stains of blood on his clothes.

'July! You have been fighting again. Siss, a man of your age and with a grown daughter still fights like a small boy. And you Ndala have come here to encourage my husband to that bashimanyana, boy's work! I thought you were more sensible than he!'

She spat on the floor and went to fetch the old man who was sitting listening to the concert where Martha was to sing.

'Ntate, July has gone again to the malaita fight. His clothes are covered with blood.'

Without being asked, the old man rose and followed her to the house.

'Mabongo! Mabongo!'

'Pa?'

'You behave like a small boy.' He pointed an admonishing finger at him: 'If I had strong men here I would ask them to thrash you. Go and sleep!'

Mabongo opened the door of his room and threw himself on the bed. He felt his joints in spasm and his head ached as if it would burst into two.

The old man turned to Ndala. 'Your cousin could have been killed and then your people would have said that he was bewitched by this poor woman.'

'I am very sorry for what has happened,' said Ndala. 'The young men with whom I came had never seen him in a bout. They asked the Pretoria malaitas to attract him to the play. This is how he came to fight and if I had tried to stop him I am certain I would have left my life at the gate.'

'Your husband is still a strong man,' Ndala told Mathloare. 'He knocked out the leading Johannesburg malaita in ten minutes!'

Mrs Mabongo thought to herself that if this man had not suggested a marriage between his son and her daughter she would have chased him away from her home.

'My husband has not been at a malaita bout since I left Pretoria to join him and he told me that he had stopped. Ndala knows that his cousin was a "king" of malaitas, so he urged him to go and fight. Siss, a real gentleman does not encourage others to fight malaitas. He is not a gentleman.'

So did she talk to herself while she washed the empty tin and scales that

42

had been used in the beer drinking and, absent-mindedly, she went back to the house still talking.

She opened the door of her room and saw her husband tossing on the bed, obviously in great pain.

'Ya! It's nice after a fight. "Pinare" and a "King"! They are young and their bones are still wet. You knock them and they just fall down and wake up again and feel no pains. You think you are still young like them. They fixed you right.'

'Please woman, leave me alone!'

'Ya, I must leave you alone and now it is I who have to nurse you! A man old as you still fights like a small boy. If you are a small boy then get up and jump about like them – the malaitas – down Harrow Road.'

Mabongo pulled the blankets and covered his head. The door banged and he could hear her speaking to Ndala.

'Your cousin is in pain. Do you see what you have caused?'

'Suka mosali, go woman. It's not me. Ma-Moipone,' Ndala changed the subject, 'I would like to see Moipone before I go back. I would like my son to come and see her when he is off duty. Let me see.' He searched his inside pocket and produced a note book and turned to the last page. 'December 16, ja, it's Dingaan's Day. Ja, it will be his day off.'

Moipone's mother smiled aside and began murmuring her favourite hymn: 'Morena ona le mohau.' Without replying to his request she disappeared into her house and came out with her shoes on.

'Moipone is singing at that church. She is going to get paid. Come let us go and hear her singing.'

'Ausi Moipone has gone to Marabi again,' said Tiny to herself when she noticed that Martha was not about. 'That grandfather will tell his boy not to marry her. I wish uncle would discover where she has gone and give her a hiding like that night she arrived when everyone was snoring.'

Martha had found George waiting for her outside the hall.

'I am pleased you have come,' he said.

'George,' appealed Martha, 'my father will see us standing together here outside and suspect us. He is well known among those malaitas and he is their King. You will never dare attempt to defend yourself against him and your men will never stand against his boys. They will fight like tigers against everyone here and in the hall.'

George looked around the side of the hall at the malaita punching one another furiously. 'Ek sal my gang roep. I'll call my gang,' he said.

Hearing this, Martha drew him into the hall, and warned: 'You, George, your gang will never stand up to the malaitas. They have had medicine incised into their blood. It is not they who fight but the medicine in them. If you hit them they don't feel anything.'

'Ja,' insisted George, 'my men will stab them with a knife.'

43

'Knife! Knife!' laughed Martha, 'Malaitas can use the knife better than blue-nines. But they don't just attack people for nothing or pick-pocket them like blue-nines. They work in the kitchens and save money, not like blue-nines who spend the money they steal from the people on dagga (marijuana) and swanky suits.'

'You mean, Martha, that I am a blue-nine?'

She looked at him and gave him a broad smile.

'No darling. You have changed.' She ran her fingers along the lapels of the black suit he was wearing and adjusted the bow tie and kissed him.

'George, I love you more than when you were a Marabi player. You have changed a lot. You look like Mr Samson who teaches me singing.'

Martha took her position in the middle of the stage and George, who was already at the piano, began running his thick fingers deftly along the keyboard.

> U ndiyeshilani sithando – sami.
> U ndishiyela zweni lobu khoboka.
> Mina nawe sidibeni e marabini,
> U ndisheyelani sithando – sami.

Ndala's tears ran freely down his cheeks.

'I thought I heard my sister's voice! God can make wonders. Her whole frame of body is Sarai my sister.'

Martha's mother exclaimed, for she had heard that name and knew that it was she whom July was supposed to have married. 'My own daughter, Moipone, looks like the woman who was to be married to the man who married me! I hate to think about it.'

Ndala said, 'Sephai, my son, must make haste to marry her before that boy who was playing the piano gets her spoiled. You hear me Ma-Moipone?'

But she was not paying attention to what he was saying.

'Sarai! This foolish man sees in Moipone a face that looks like his sister's! He wants her for his son and then the whole Ndala and Mabongo family will have the same blood brought back to them. Siss, his uncle does not like me but I have borne them a child that looks like them. I am a fair woman. I have not given July a womb of another man. Other women cheat their lovers by going with other men and when they are pregnant they say to the man they love most: "You have spoiled me." And the poor man says: "Hau, I have not slept with you for a long time. How can it be myself?" And the woman cries and says to him: "Ja, you say it is not you because you have a lot of girls." And the poor man just says "all right".'

The people of the early times believed that all sorrow vanishes with the fall of the night and is turned away somewhere among the dead, and the

44

gods come to soothe the pains of all who have not offended them during the day, and guard their bodies against all evils. It was not so with Mabongo. He had gone to bed on the old man's instructions after his wife had cursed him for going to the malaita bout and coming back with bloodstains on his clothes.

'Women can cast an evil spell on one,' the old man had often told Mabongo. 'Never argue with them even if you know you are right. Ke baloi. – They are witches.'

July's joints – ankles, knees, shoulders, elbows, knuckles – all twitched like ants on a grass-roofed house. His body burned like a farmer's baking oven and his breath smelt hot and had a sour flavour.

'Ntate Moipone.' His wife shook him. 'Are you sick?'

'I don't know.'

'Your body and breath is too hot.'

'I don't know.'

'Moipone,' her mother pulled the blankets from Martha's covered head. 'Go and wake your grandfather. Your father is very sick. Tell him not to waste time.'

Martha got up and went next door returning with the old man.

'There have been many people here during the day and their feet were too hot. That is the reason Mabongo has become so sick.' He spread water from a tin with his hands over the room and let Mabongo gulp the remainder. 'He will have a sleep now.'

On the instructions of the old man, Mathloare slept with Martha on the floor.

The first cock crowed, to remind the last sleepers that it was late. Mathloare heard July snoring and as she listened sleep forced itself on her against her wish to keep a vigil on her husband.

'Moipone.' She shook her daughter violently.

'Ma.'

'You say, "Ma", you don't even know how your father slept. You will sleep on top of your child. Go and make fire, your father must be very hungry. He did not eat last night.'

Martha listlessly stretched her arms and yawned.

'You lazy child. It's about time your father should have left for work.'

'Is he not gone yet?' inquired Martha.

'Gone? My child, your father is very sick.'

'Ma,' began Martha, 'I had a vision last night.' She looked at her father who was still asleep but appeared to be hearing. 'I saw a man. He looked older than my grandfather, Mapena. But he was tall and his body was broad. He wore across his shoulders coloured beads and was dressed below in leopard skins. From a large lapa (compound) he walked towards a kraal for cattle and sheep and goats. Then he turned away from the kraal and the home and covered his face and sobbed like a child: "My

45

son, my son." Then the vision turned to town. I saw a man also dressed in skins, with a baboon head and with an ox tail in his right hand. Behind him came a man a little older than he, carrying a suitcase which seemed to contain medicines. I did not see how this man was dressed and behind him came a girl who appeared to be the wife of the man who was leading them and she was dressed in light calico cloth with a skin dress on her loins. She carried a home-made mat embroidered with beads. The man who led them came towards our house and just when he was about to enter you woke me up.'

'You have seen your father.' Mabongo dropped his head back on the pillow and looked pensively at his daughter.

'Ndala has bewitched us!' exclaimed his wife. 'How can Martha see your father and your home after he has been here? He wants you to die so that he can let his son marry Moipone for nothing. He has left his boloi in the house and carried Moipone to your place. Oh Morena! His baboon has been riding my daughter the whole night. I must get a Zulu doctor to chase it away.' She sobbed.

'Ma, you are making my father worse. There is no truth in your idea that a baboon rode me the whole night. My father's people are mine and they are my gods, so they must visit me. It may be that it was an admonition that I should not refuse to marry my father's cousin.'

Mabongo smiled and beckoned his daughter to come nearer him. He laid his hand on her head, saying, 'I shall be well by tomorrow. Your grandfather prayed to his great-grandfather, Mathathakanye, to bring you to him and his crying is for joy at having seen you, because he does not know you. As for the other people you say: the leader was a doctor, the other man a medicine carrier, the doctor's wife was given to him on the way by her parents because they could not pay him. The mat she was carrying is a sign of agreement that she will make bed for her husband. If I am ever away and very sick this doctor, who turned away when your mother woke you, will know how to prevent your mother from interfering with his business. When your grandfather beats a drum doctors from all over the country sneeze to find out where the sick person is.'

That afternoon clouds gathered and by the time the men began arriving home from work rain was already falling. When the supper was ready it began to pour.

'Your gods have shown you to your grandparents, my child, and this rain is brought by you to your people to wash the hot feet that caused your father's sickness.' So said the old man to Martha when he returned from work. 'I am not a doctor like your father but I can help in small sickness,' he told Mabongo, and turning to Martha's mother he told her to prepare boiling water and get two heavy blankets.

Mabongo undressed and the old man threw two hot stones into the boiling water. Covered with the blankets Mabongo sat over the bath of

46

seething water. Sweat ran like a shower of rain from his body and he puffed and puffed against the heat of the smouldering stones and boiling water.

'It is khumama – rheumatism. Go to work tomorrow,' the old man told him.

4

ROOIVELDT DAIRIES, WHERE Mabongo had worked for twenty years, since he was fifteen, was one of the largest dairies in the country. Starting as a small shop employing not more than six workers, it had grown to employ about a hundred and to control many smaller dairies on the Reef and in Pretoria. It still, however, to a great extent used animal-drawn transport. Motor transport was confined to fetching milk from the farmers and supplying the smaller dairies. The process of filling milk bottles was done by hand.

Mabongo had been transferred from the Pretoria depot after Rooiveldt Dairies opened its headquarters in Johannesburg. He was in charge of the African staff and his duties, although not defined in law, included: 'driving animal-drawn vehicle', 'delivery by bicycle to customers', 'supervision of all employees, other than whites', and 'cleaning and filling of bottles.'

His contract of service was determined by the laws controlling the employment of 'Natives' in the urban areas. These laid down rules on such matters as the registering of the Native with the Pass Office and the signing of his Pass every month, not later than the seventh day of each month, and the paying of a sum of two shillings every month by the employer. 'The employer or the Native shall give notice to terminate service on the first day of the month and the employer shall grant the Native a special pass to travel at night for the purpose of visiting or carrying out the duties of the employer.'

Rooiveldt Dairies had been known to its customers by a special name in its early days: Tenka-Tenka – Fly Dairy. But it prospered in spite of its unpleasant nickname.

There were older employees than Mabongo, men who had gone without wages when business was bad. The proprietor, Mr Tereplasky, had at first faced more prosperous rivals who had used bicycles for deliveries, while he could afford only hand-pushed carts. He had been helped in the business by his wife, who made dresses in the evenings and advertised them in the shop window. The family had been frugal and had saved a large sum of money. When an old employee was retired Mr Tereplasky took him aside and thanked him by handing him some golden coins in a closed hand: 'Now, don't tell the other boys. Go out of this door. Good-bye.'

Mabongo had been engaged in the month of July.

'What is your name?'

'July, baas.'

'Alright, July, start. Can you ride a bicycle?'

July looked blankly at the interpreter.

'Tell him I shall buy a bicycle for him and he has to learn to ride it. In the mornings he will have to take the klein baas to school and fetch him in the afternoons.'

Thus Mabongo had known his employer's son from the boy's early childhood. When the dairy was expanded and the headquarters moved to Johannesburg, the old man retired from active management and handed over to his son. Mabongo was transferred to the headquarters to be induna (overseer) to the African staff and to drive an animal-drawn vehicle. Mr Tereplasky, junior, learned much of the business from him.

'You are my father's old boy,' he would say, patting him on the shoulders. 'You shall never be out of work.'

The day following his illness a trade union organizer came to visit Mabongo. He advised him to call a white doctor to find out if he was fit to resume duties. The doctor advised him that it would be safer for him to remain at home for a week. 'I will give you a letter to say you were not able to work.'

Mabongo reported for duty the following week at four o'clock in the morning and waited outside while the workers who slept on the premises were getting ready. One of them went to wake the white foreman who lived not far from the dairy.

'So at last you have decided to come,' said the foreman. 'You stayed away for a whole week. Who did you think would do your work? Don't touch anything, wait for the big boss.'

So he sat on a stone at the entrance of the stable while the foreman and the new employee tried to control the horse which was stamping and snorting at them. 'Hoo, you black Sam!' Mabongo heard the foreman screaming to the horse.

One of the horses, on seeing him, trotted to the stable door, stopped suddenly, pawed the ground and reared jubilantly, then lowered his head and sniffed him. He patted its jaws and pressed his cheek against it.

'Leave that horse! Get out of here! You think the baas does not know that you have given these horses native herbs so that they will hate other people. Get out or I will kick you out!'

'If you dare even lift your foot you will wake up in hospital.' Mabongo looked at him defiantly and stood arms akimbo.

Mr Tereplasky arrived at nine o'clock and went straight to his office, followed by his foreman: 'July has come, Sir.'

'I have had enough of him – milk not fetched in time, bottles not properly washed, horses not fed on time and giving trouble. I have lost enough money through him. Tell him to come in.'

He looked Mabongo up and down. 'You are a nice chap. Give me your pass.' But instead of his pass, Mabongo handed him the note. After reading it he returned it to him. 'I have seen too many of these. Give me your pass!'

'Baas,' Mabongo remonstrated, 'I worked for your father for a very long time. I took you to school every morning and sold milk in the streets afterwards. Sometimes I went without pay for weeks. You asked the old baas to transfer me from Pretoria and I taught you the business. You are rich now but I am still poor. You buy a new motor car every year and I still have to go on a bicycle.'

He lowered his right hand to his side. 'Take – there's my pass!' He flung it on to the table and waited.

'Mr Rambuck, you stand there like a fool and listen to this kaffir insulting me. Can't you push him outside?'

Mabongo pushed Mr Rambuck aside and went to the door. 'Sign my pass now and pay me all that is due to me. I shall leave your premises and never again put my foot here.'

'There is your money for the whole week and another for notice pay. I am sorry you had to drink so much and get sick. You should have sent your wife to the farms instead of staying in the dirty yards where skokiaan is brewed.' He feigned to be laughing, 'I hope you get another good baas like me You see I shall give you a very good reference – that you were " a very good boy, honest and hardworking" and you left of your own accord.'

He handed Mabongo his money, counting each gold sovereign by placing it on the desk separately and then taking all the pieces again and counting them into his hands.

'July, you have been a very nice boy, here's your reference. If you don't get work, come back and I may be able to take you on again. I want you to go and suffer a little bit.'

Thoughts raced through Mabongo's head as he left the dairy.

'You can't trust a white man. You work for him all your life and tomorrow he sacks you like a new boy. Makgato should have sent them all into the sea. There is no sense in my cousin saying they will one day treat us like brothers. They suck your blood and when it is finished they say "voetsak".

'His father and mother were very poor. They slept in the back room of the dairy, and Tiba, their servant, told me that Lazar, this baas, was cared for by his wife and slept with them like their own child and cried the whole night, and they never had sleep whilst his mother and father snored.'

He clenched his fist and turned his face towards the dairy: 'If I ever find you alone I will wring your neck. I made you rich and you push me out of your dairy like rubbish.

'The old baas was very good. I saw him giving that man of Pietersburg

49

a lot of money and telling him not to tell us about it, and the old missus gave him some dresses for his wife and children and bought him plenty of bread and a tin of syrup.'

He trudged slowly to the Pass Office to get a special pass to 'seek' work. 'I have not been to the Pass Office for many years.' He counted on his fingers and repeated twice on both hands: 'Before Moipone was born. Today she is already a woman and about to be married.'

It was before noon and the officials had not gone for lunch. There was still a queue of job-seekers and African police of the Native Affairs Department were screaming at the tops of their voices: 'Line up, you sepolopoko – stupid! You think this is your house. Next one – ngena lapa – queue here.'

A fat white official with spectacles halfway down his nose looked at the job seekers askance: ' Trek jou hoed af.' The hat landed a few feet outside the office before the man had a chance to take it off.

'Don't you know that this is the Pass Office?'

The queue police cuffed the man: 'Pas op – take care!'

Mabongo went up to the policeman who was standing at the main entrance: 'Where can I get a special?'

'What special? There is a special for travelling, a special for a visit, a special to go out at night and a special to seek work.'

'I want a special to seek work.'

The policeman looked at his watch. 'Don't you know that this is lunch-time?' He flung the gate closed and locked it. 'Wait there until two o'clock.'

More men arrived while Mabongo was waiting and the police also arrived and began asking for passes.

'Waar is jou pass, jou? Hoekom is hy nie reg nie?' And a man was flung into the pick-up van.

'And you – where's your pass? Reg – right.'

By the time the gate opened half the job-seekers had been taken by the police.

'Kenga Satane – it is a devil's place.' Mabongo shook his head.

'Ngena, ngena.' Young and old men rushed at the gate, jostling each other.

There were still half the men inside waiting to be served. Some wore hungry faces, some were in dilapidated clothes, and some appeared to have spent the night in their clothes.

'These are the men just released from prison.'

'What could they have gone to prison for?'

'You ask what they could have gone to prison for! Don't you know we Africans can be arrested at any time. Your children are never sure that you will return home.'

'Hey, you two talk too much. Get out of the queue.' A policeman wielded a knobkerrie at them. 'Puma!'

50

The queue moved slowly to the officials who at times sat looking at the job-seekers and laughing: 'What dirty passes are these? Why don't you keep your pass clean?'

'Next,' an official looked at the pass, 'How long did you work for Rooiveldt Dairies?'

Mabongo spread out all his fingers twice and again spread one hand. 'A very long time.'

'Ja baas.'

'Why did they sack you from work?'

'Ek was siek – I was sick.'

The official stopped writing. 'I shall send you to the chief. Escort!' A portly African policeman saluted: 'Yebo nkosi.'

'Take this man to the chief, then wait for him and bring him back.'

'Yebo nkosi.'

Mabongo followed the escort down a passage. The policeman knocked lightly on a door and walked in, followed by Mabongo. He placed the pass and a note from the official on the large desk and stood at attention. The Chief looked at the note and then at the pass and shook his head.

'Why did they sack you after you had worked for them for so many years?'

'I was sick.'

The Chief took a telephone directory book and rang up Rooiveldt Dairies.

'Yes, I see.'

He turned to Mabongo: 'You natives think you can do as you like when you have worked for a white man for a long time.'

He scribbled a note and stamped it: 'Take him back.'

Back in the main office the clerk told him: 'The chief says he will give you a special for fourteen days, but if you don't find work within those days you will be sent home.'

'I have got children here in Johannesburg.'

'It's not our indaba.'

He left the pass office dismayed. 'White men's law has no regard for black men's children.'

It was almost sunset when he got to his cousin's place of work to tell him what had happened. 'My cousin knows clever people. They might help me,' he thought.

He found Ndala sitting outside the shop with other neighbouring workers.

'Hau Cousy! What do you want at this time?'

'I am from the pass office. I am out of work.'

'Hau Cousy, you are out of work?' And he related what had happened: 'Moipone dreamed on Monday when I was sick that her grandfather had turned his face from his kraal and cattle post and cried "my son, my son!" I then explained to her that he was referring to her because he had not

51

seen her. But it was a lie; my father wanted me and has seen through his ditaola that I was ill.'

'The gods have turned their faces away from you,' agreed Ndala, 'my uncle's visit to Moipone was a picture of the gods showing anger that Moipone was not borne by Sarai.'

Mabongo blushed and bent his head at the mention of Sarai. He thought to himself: 'Could my cousin still be disappointed at me for not having married his sister or is he jealous of Moipone resembling his sister – stoutness, heavy voice, prominent breasts and a man-shaped forehead?'

'Cousy,' resumed Ndala after a long silence, 'don't think that I hate your wife because you did not marry my sister, but the gods have made it ka boomo that your daughter should look like my sister so that you shall never forget that you have not listened to them.'

'I am very sorry about not listening to the gods and if Sarai was not yet married I would take her as a second wife.'

'To make the gods forgive you Moipone must be married to one of the family and you must allow the marriage to be managed by my mother and you must allow her to decide the number of cattle to be paid.'

'Why should Rakgadi decide bogadi?'

'Because she would have received bogadi from uncle if you had married Sarai.'

'Will my father not be against your mother taking all the bogadi?'

'Uncle has no right to object because you, his son, have disappointed the gods. My uncle has fears of the gods because they may take away all his cleverness about bones, herbs, boloi, and if he lost all these he would become stupid, go about naked and eat masepa.'

'Perhaps I also am about to go naked and eat masepa,' thought Mabongo to himself.

'Cousy, I see you are worried. The gods will not make you stupid because you are not a doctor like my uncle. But they will make madimabe: you have lost a job where you were employed since you left farm work. It was from your first wages for that farm work that you gave my mother money to buy a dress for Sarai and my mother still has the change and the piece of cloth she bought. Last year when I got home for Christmas she produced the change and the piece of cloth and said: "My brother's son has forgotten to buy another dress for my daughter and I am keeping this money for him".'

Mabongo cried aloud like a woman: 'Yo me, Yo.'

'July, I am your uncle and I must slaughter a white goat to wash away your madimabe. When my uncle is not present I take his place. I shall buy it before Christmas and have it slaughtered at your home. I shall have you smeared with the inside wastes and you and Moipone shall not eat the meat because the gods are against a person of the same blood taking part in the feast during the washing of their sins. Moipone is the pure blood of Mathathakanye and if her first born is a boy that boy remains with

52

the grandfather until he dies, and then he takes everything that belonged to his grandfather – ditaola, herbs, and leruo.'

'What about the marriage of Moipone to your son? Will it not cause Rakgadi to object because she can't take bogadi from her own grandson?'

'No, when my son marries your daughter, my mother will instruct the people who will be sent to find out how many cattle are required. Because she still has the piece of cloth and the change from Sarai's dress, you must give back to her the cattle she would have got if you had married Sarai. Then she will take the cloth and the money to where the bones of her grandfathers are buried and leave them there, and you shall become a man again. The white man who chased you away today will come to look for you because the people who buy his milk will say: "I don't want your milk any more. That boy who brings milk is no good." And still when he has changed the boy they will say: "That one is also no good".'

'Why will they not like the new boys?'

'Because the gods will go to the dairy and put madimabe in the dairy if they do not find you there. The goat that I will slaughter will make the gods cast their shadows on you and the white man, and he will send someone to call you back to work and he will say, "I am very sorry, my old boy. The old baas came to me in a dream and said, "I want July".'

'Keago leboga – I thank you.'

Mabongo arrived home at an unusually late hour. He used the Angle Road entrance because he no longer had the bicycle which he had had to chain on the baths heaped in the corner at the main entrance to the cottage. and by using the other entrance he avoided the mud in the yard.

'Your father is coming through the back. What could have happened to his bicycle?'

When Mabongo came in he threw himself onto the bed and remained quiet for some time.

'Are you feeling sick again?' asked his wife.

'I am not sick.'

'Then what is it?'

He buried his face in his hands: 'Moipone, my child, your dream was very bad. You have gods with you. They tell beforehand of what will happen. It has happened to me today.' He paused and asked for water. 'I have never looked for work but today I shall learn to look for it.'

The old man had been listening to the conversation.

'Have you been sacked?'

'Yes. You can't trust a white man. You put him on your back like a little brother and work for his father, and when his father is too old to work or he is dead you work for the son and teach him all the work. He gets rich and buys a nice house and motor cars. When you get sick and cannot come to work, he says: "You think you can do as you like! Here's your pass".'

53

'My child, don't worry. He will want you again. You know his work better than all the workers. Your baas is still too young. He believes all he is told by workers who are jealous of you and he wants to show you that he is a white man and you a black who can do nothing to a white man. If you go to Mohle to report that he chased you away from work because you were sick, they will say: "You think you are clever to say a white man is wrong. Puma!" But they won't come to help him when nobody can harness the horses and the white women don't get their milk before the baas goes to work. If your baas goes to the Native Commissioner and says "I want a good boy who can work in the milk", they will say: "Go and try that one." Don't worry, my boy.'

After the old man had gone back to his house Mabongo told his wife that he had been at his cousin's place.

'He is going to come and take off madimabe.'

'How can he take your bad luck when he is not your uncle?'

'He said he stands in the place of my uncle when he is not here.'

'You are a bushman. You don't understand the laws. You are his uncle because you are his uncle's son. He should come to you when he has got madimabe. You have stayed too long in town and don't know the laws. O se tlaela sa monna – you are a fool of a man. How can Ndala be an uncle to you?'

'He said that if he doesn't wash me I shall get more madimabe, and that when Moipone is married all her bogadi will go to his mother.'

'Oareng? I must get into pains for other women and go for nine moons and sit the whole night without sleep. Molimo, they will get it when I am dead. I am going to call my brother to take the cattle. You have not paid anything for me and you have no right to receive the bogadi. You must first pay mine.'

'Ma, you trouble my father,' said Martha. 'I have never seen any uncle from your home yet today you say he must come and take my bogadi. I can rather go with a man for nothing.'

Her mother picked up a wooden porridge spoon and landed it on her head. 'I have long seen that you have made yourself the woman of this house. I shall walk out and you stay. Every time I talk to your father you jump into my mouth like a fly. You are a woman. Get into the blankets!'

It was two weeks since Mabongo had been discharged from work and he went to the Pass Office for another special pass.

The rent had been paid with the wages for the week and part of the notice pay had been used for paying other debts. Martha and her mother continued to take in washing and looked forward to being paid at the end of the month.

'If I don't find a job before the end of the month my family is going to starve and the rent collector will throw us out,' Mabongo thought to himself as he stood in the long queue of job-seekers that twisted round the building like a snake. 'But what I fear most is that the white man giving out specials will chase me away and refuse to give me a special pass. I have no house at home, no cattle, no ploughing fields. Where shall I go?'

It took hours to reach the special issuing officer. But when he got to the top of the queue he was told: 'You were given two weeks to look for work. Pas op, this is the last one. If you don't find work you will be sent home.'

On the Saturday afternoon of the second week after Mabongo had been discharged, Ndala arrived at 26 Staib Street, Doornfontein, leading a white goat by a rope. On seeing him Tiny jumped about for joy that it was a magadi for Martha.

'Ausi Moipone is getting married.'

Ndala stood erect in an open area behind the Molefe yard holding the goat by its horns.

'If, when I lay my knife on its neck it does not cry, the gods shall not answer our prayers,' he told Mabongo.

Holding the knife tightly between his teeth, he turned the goat's face towards the East and murmured inaudible words, understood only by his cousin.

'Take ye gods of Mabongo and Mathathakanye. Wash all that is bad in your child. Sleep (peace) for your child.'

The goat bleated an agonized cry.

'Yo!' cried Tiny. 'They kill Ausi Moipone's bogadi.'

'I am your uncle because my uncle is not present. You are my uncle when I am madimabe. Moipone is an angel for her grandfather because you have no boy child. Come nearer my child.'

Moipone went down on her knees and Ndala smeared her face with undigested grass and bid her drink the blood from the skin.

'Get down on your knees.' Mabongo got on his knees. 'Robalang ngoana oa lona – give peace to your child.'

Mr Tereplasky arrived at his office earlier than usual and demanded to see the foreman as promptly as possible.

The phone rang: 'Rooiveldt Dairies.'

'I have received your account for more milk than you delivered. I rang your clerk last week to say that milk deliveries had been very irregular and late, arriving after my husband and children had left for work and school. . . . '

The caller banged the receiver down.

'Hello? Is that the Rooiveldt Dairies? This is the Braamfontein Station. Your men have left two four-gallon cans of milk on the station last night.'

Mr Tereplasky flung himself out of the office.

The telephone rang again.

He ran back and picked up the receiver. 'Rooiveldt Dairies.'

A hoarse voice gurgled some incomprehensible words: 'Dit is Marshall Square,' and changed into English. 'The Rooiveldt Dairies trolley cart has collided with a municipal bus and we had to shoot one of the horses because its leg was broken.'

'Rambuck! Rambuck!' Tereplasky ran again out of the office as if stung by a bee. 'You have ruined me! Thirty years of hard work has gone to hell in two weeks. . . . '

Mr Rambuck had not yet heard that the trolley had collided with a bus and a horse had been shot, nor did he know about the milk cans left at the station.

'Hy is mal,' he thought.

'Mr Rambuck, you made me get rid of July. And now I can see the reason. He understood the work better than you. And you felt that you could not be under a black man. I was a fool to listen to your advice. I am giving you one month's notice.'

The cleansing ceremony ended on Sunday night. People from the yard and friends from the suburbs were given strict instructions not to treat the feast like a wedding. There was no eating off a table, no spoons were used, all the bones were burned so that no dog should pick up a bone. The people ate in groups, no person was to eat by himself.

Mabongo and his daughter were the only people who did not partake in the feast.

'You have sipped its blood and the rest I spilt into the earth for badimo to drink. If you, as the unfortunate person, take part in the festival and eat the meat, all your madimabe will come back into you.'

Ndala did not know well the art of diagnosing from bones but he had a good knowledge of herbs, for he had often searched for a certain root and when he found it his mother or uncle had told him for what sickness it was. In his boyhood he had nursed his uncle's patients and had learned to know which herbs give the best cure. There were other people too who came to the doctor, for strong medicines against enemies, for finding work, to make them liked, feared or respected by people, love medicines, luck medicines, and many other herbs believed to have some effect on human beings or animals.

The European suburbs, sparsely populated, offered a lot of roots to those who knew them, and Ndala spent Sundays and holidays searching for them. He became known to shop workers and domestic workers.

'My man wants a child, can you help me?'

'I want Mary, can you give a moratiso?'

'I want work.'

Ndala encountered no difficulties in getting the right herb and his clients often came back to thank him.

'Sethlare gase legogoe – don't thank the receiving of medicine.'

All his patients or clients came to know the custom that medicine is never thanked. They paid the requested amount and walked away without a word, particularly in the case of a herb wanted for love.

56

He turned away all those who wanted a medicine to bewitch.

'I don't want customers who want medicine to loya other people. I want to help, not to kill or cause harm to other people. I am not a witch doctor.'

After the cleansing ceremony he gave his cousin a herb which goes soft when the weather is cloudy! 'Lira ga libone. This medicine will guard you against your enemies, no one will attack you. Keep it always in your pocket. Here is molomo monate: it will make many friends for you and when you look for work keep a piece in your mouth. And here is maime: it will make other people respect you. If your baas calls you back to work smear it on your eyebrows and look him straight in the face. He will say "I am sorry".'

Mr Tereplasky took over the work which had been done by Rambuck: checking the milk at the station, filling bottles, going over the customers list with the men who did the rounds, instructing the clerk to issue notices to all the customers asking them to notify the office immediately of late deliveries. To satisfy himself he even stuck postage stamps on the letters and went himself to the post office to fetch the post. If there were any returned letters from customers who had moved he searched for their new addresses. He stood at the stable door to see that the horses were properly fed and brushed. In the evenings, after work, he took home all the account books and statements and got his wife and daughter to go through them and put aside any queries to take to the auditors.

Mr Rambuck was given the duties of seeing that the compound was kept clean and that there were no flies to be seen in the dairy premises. 'If he does not like the work, he can leave before his notice month expires. I have had enough of him since he got rid of my father's old boy.'

Mr Tereplasky often came home exhausted.

'You are going to ruin your health, Lazar. Why don't you get July back? It won't cost you anything to say: "I am sorry old man – come and work. I will pay you more money." Or to treat him as a human being and give him due respect.'

'What respect must I give him? Do you mean I must call him mister?'

'Why not?' interjected his wife. 'If you feel too proud to call "mister" then call him Mabongo and stop calling any of the men "boys".'

'Have you become a friend of the Natives?'

'Lazar! We must learn to respect them so that we can live in peace with them.'

'Alright Hannah. I'll get Mabongo tonight.'

He got into his car and drove to the Dairy which was situated to the south of Johannesburg, in the working class area. When he arrived he called to one of his employees: 'Frans, get into the car. I must get Mabongo tonight.' He drove back in the direction from which he had come –

towards the Northern area which was largely a middle class area except for Doornfontein which was a 'black spot'.

It was between nine and ten when the car's lights shone into the Molefe Yard where Mabongo lived. After ascertaining the number, which was painted on a corrugated iron gate, Frans got out of the car to ask a woman who was still cooking outside if Mabongo still lived there.

'Go round to Angle Road,' she told him, 'the yard is full of mud and the baas will spoil his trousers.'

By swerving the car towards the east, then turning slightly to the south Mr Tereplasky and Frans reached the Angle Road entrance.

Mabongo had seen the headlights and knew that it was his employer's car.

'My baas is coming.'

'You say your baas is coming and do nothing to get maime and tlokoa-latsela? You stand there like a fool!'

Mathloare took out the herbs and urged her husband to prepare himself as Ndala had directed.

Frans again got out of the car and went to knock at the main door. On receiving no answer he walked into the dark passage and knocked on the door of the Mabongos' room.

'Tsena,' called Mrs Mabongo. 'Hau! Hau! Where do you come from late?'

'I have come with the baas. He wants Mabongo to come and work now.'

Mr Tereplasky, after waiting some time in the car, got out and called to July. He came into the dimly lit room saying:

'Come Mr Mabongo, I am sorry. Come to work and I will pay you more money and you will never be sacked again. Come now, don't be a woman.'

During this discourse Mabongo stood erect and looked his former employer straight in the face. He kept pushing out his breath which had the smell of the piece of molomo monate.

'Are these your two wives?' asked Mr Tereplasky and then fixed his eyes on Martha and thought to himself what a beautiful wife Mabongo had.

'No, it is my child.'

'Then she must come and work for the missus.'

'I am a singer,' replied Martha in perfect English.

'Then you are no good to work in kitchens.'

'I do any kind of work. I am only engaged at this time because there is going to be a competition and I must practice hard in order to win the prize.'

'How old are you?'

Martha fumbled on her fingers: 'Sixteen.'

'You look too big for sixteen. I thought you were twenty-two or more.'

Turning to Mabongo, Mr Tereplasky again appealed to him to return to work.

'Tsamac le lekgoa le – go with the white man,' shouted Mabongo's wife as he pretended to be unwilling to go with his former employer. So Mabongo gave in.

'I have sacked Rambuck,' Mr Tereplasky told him as they drove back to the dairy. 'He told me lies about you: that you bewitched the horses so that they could not be handled by the other boys.'

Mabongo blushed and thought of the root still in his mouth and suspected that his employer may have noticed the black stuff on his eyelids.

'I have lost a lot of money in the two weeks you were away. Your favourite mare has been shot by the police because its leg was broken in an accident; milk has been left on the station and gone sour and the customers have refused to pay their accounts because their milk has not been delivered. The missus will be glad that you have come back.'

'My cousin is a great doctor,' Mabongo said to himself.

The car left the main route to the south and went through dimly lighted streets, passing houses where windows and doors appeared to be well secured against intruders.

Mr Tereplasky noticed for the first time the contrast between the southern and northern areas: 'Bright lights there and windows big enough to allow light through and a night watchman to see that nobody comes to the house. . . . '

Mabongo wasted no time when they got to the dairy. He went to the stable, at first feeling sad at the loss of Molly, his favourite mare. But the other horse, Jim, stamped its hooves and snorted in joy at seeing its old friend again. The new horse, still unnamed, looked blankly at the stranger who had entered the stable. After patting Jim, Mabongo moved to the new horse and stretched out his hand as if in salutation. The horse answered by rearing and stamping the ground.

'Medrai!' He called its name aloud and the horse pricked up its ears.

5

DINGAAN'S DAY, the day for Martha and Ndala's son to meet, had arrived. It was soon after Mabongo had been re-engaged and Ndala, on hearing of this, was proud that his muti could work mysteries. He hurried to his son's working place to 'prepare' the young man's body not to fail the love of Martha.

'I have been able to get her father back to work. Now I must prepare you to win the love of his daughter. She is the pure blood of my uncle and the cattle must go back to the kraal.'

As he was saying these words, he produced a small bag of porcupine skin, bidding his son to sit on the floor. He scattered a number of bones and began praising them: 'Morekola litaba, rekola badimo, balumele ngoana ona tsela – the releaser of matters, release the gods to allow this child to see his way clear.' He shifted a small bone which appeared to be that of an ape or monkey: 'Let the elephant pass.'

After a short silence he exclaimed: 'Ahasa . . . the badimo have agreed amongst themselves. They say the woman is yours. They have borne her for you. Take this, it is the medicine of the badimo. They will speak for you if you are afraid.' He handed his son a yellow root: 'Moratiso oa badimo – love of the gods.'

Sephai had never known his father to throw bones: 'I did not know you could throw bones, pa.'

'I don't want people to know, because other doctors will test me to see if I am strong enough. I only throw bones for myself to find out my ways. You are myself, my own blood.'

Then Ndala left, for it was still morning and his son had stolen from work when his employer, Mrs McDonald, went to the shop.

'You haven't cleaned the bedrooms. What have you been doing?' demanded Mrs McDonald when she returned.

'My father came to see me,' answered Sephai.

'I won't let you go till you finish your work.'

On hearing that he would certainly be released when he finished, Sephai dashed through his work. In less than the time he usually took, he had finished making the beds, polishing the floors, cleaning the lounge, bathroom, pantry and corridor. By ten o'clock, teatime, he had finished the kitchen.

'Is your father going to get you a wife, John?' inquired the little European boy who had overheard Ndala talking of 'mosali', which he understood to mean 'woman'.

'Ja, klein baas, little baas. Nice girl there in location. Fat one. So big.' He spread his hands wide over his hips. 'Ja, so big here,' and brought them to his chest. 'Sing nice,' and he opened his mouth as wide as he could. 'Dance so,' and shuffled his feet elegantly on the floor.

'But you haven't got cattle to buy her.'

'What you talk about? Me no cattle? You no cattle! Missus buy milk in the street. Me no buy milk. Piccanin milk twenty cattle. Milk too much, give pigs. You nothing. Buy milk street.'

'Why do you work for us if you have a lot of cattle?'

'Die policeman come say "Tax kaffir"! Must go work.'

'Why don't you sell some of your cattle to pay tax?'

'Venkele rob. Shopkeepers are thieves. Better come work for tax. Cattle plenty me buy wife. Ah! That location one nice and fat. Next month me go home with my new woman and go and make piccanin.'

Mrs Mabongo had noted well the date when Ndala's son would come and court her daughter. Unknown to her husband, she had been to her private doctor – also to prepare her Moipone for marriage: 'Men are kalachane, deceivers. If you want them to marry you, you must tjisa them with love root.'

The doctor to whom she had gone did not throw bones like Ndala. He placed in front of her a small calabash with a string fastened to a stick standing inside it. He stuck the string with a porcupine thorn and began to sing a mournful song:

'Badimo ba borare nchang litabe – gods of my fathers let out the secrets.'

His face was sad and stern as he beat the string and sang and sang:

'Bo papa lebo ma balileng – what have my fathers and mothers done? Talk Baroka. Talk Baroka.'

He beat the string, beat it and hummed the song. His deep baritone voice echoed around the thatched hut where he and the woman seeking marriage for her daughter sat – all alone to hear the secrets.

She had gone out of town to find a good doctor who did not cheat or tell lies – a doctor who still had connection with the gods. She trusted this doctor because he had made her win her husband from many women over twenty years ago when she was still young and Moipone was not yet born. This doctor had now a lot of experience, and his baroka, small insects that live in the calabash, had accumulated, and those which had died had left a lot of knowledge to the younger ones. They never rushed to tell before they had examined the patient carefully and been convinced that she had a serious taba to smell out.

The doctor stopped the beating but kept on singing. A murmur ascended from the calabash. It was more sorrowful than the doctor's. The words were thin but audible, then a still thinner voice was heard:

'You have come to know about the marriage of Moipone your daughter. Haaaa!' It laughed spitefully. 'Your daughter has another man. Ndala is a doctor. He fears other doctors. His son loves your daughter. Next moon he is going home to tell his mother to send some people to look for a wife for him. Haaa! Mosali, you have no child.'

Then there was a murmur again and this time a mournful voice called out:

'Mathloare, Mathloare, your child is going to say "No".'

When Mrs Mabongo heard this last word she wept and wept and asked the doctor whether she could not stop her daughter from saying "No".'

He fetched a bag of medicine and placed it in front of the calabash. As before he beat the string and hummed the song:

'Kgapha! Thapo ea Badimo. Kgaptha! Thapo ea Badimo. Move! The string of the gods.'

Ten voices repeated the words.

The doctor took from one of his bags raw reed-cotton and bade the woman coil a string. When it was completed he took out fat with his finger nails from ten horns of different animals and mixed it together and ran it along the string. Then he rubbed it into a skin that looked like that of a mouse:

61

'Wash your hands after you touch it,' he warned. 'Take this and tie it around the hips of your daughter. Whoever touches her will die immediately, with his hand having shrunk. It will make her smell like all the animals whose fat is on it and no man will want to touch her.'

Mrs Mabongo gave another wail: 'What about Ndala's son?'

'Wait woman, I have not yet finished.'

He took out a claw that looked like that of a big bird, from another bag.

'Inside this is medicine that will make Ndala's son run mad if he touches her bosom. If he touches her on Dingaan's Day he will not sleep that night. It stops the smell. Tell her to smear it round her neck, but only when the boy comes. Monday, Tuesday, Wednesday will be Dingaan's Day. Hide everything from your husband and after he has gone to work tomorrow prepare her for Wednesday. She must stay at home.'

Mrs Mabongo arrived home late, looking very tired. She found that her husband had already returned from work.

'Where have you been the whole day and this night?' he asked her.

'Au! Ntate Moipone. This missus made me wash everything in the house. If I was not afraid of you I would have slept there. Here is an old shirt she gave me for bansela.'

'You stayed so late because you do not like my people. You know that my cousin's child is coming on Wednesday and yet you have not bothered to speak to your daughter on how she should treat him.'

'Au! Ntate Moipone. Should I tell Moipone how a man must be treated? Metlolo, if a woman has to tell her child how to sleep with a man.'

She unpacked the parcels she had bought on the way from the doctor to make her husband believe that she had been to do washing and the white people had given her vegetables and scraps of bread.

'I have gone to look for food and you want me to stay home so that tomorrow you can call me a lazy woman. God has given me hands to plough for myself.'

'If your child behaves like that to a man, by my father's badimo, she will be sent back to her home. Women are not allowed to be out of the house after sunset. They would find their children fallen in the fire. Your child is just like you – look, she is still running about in the street. How can she be a mother? She has taken after you. I am sorry that I married a woman like you.'

'Yes, I knew that you would say that. Sarai! Siss, rubbish! Why didn't you marry her, your Rakgadi's child? The cattle would have gone back to the kraal. Wena – you, ntate Moipone, have not married me! You paid nothing for me. Ke mosali zam oa magala – I am a free woman! You can still go and marry her!'

At this point Martha pushed open the door without knocking:

'Ma, you always quarrel with my father when some of his people come here. I shall leave this house and go and work in the kitchens, and when I find a man I shall never bring him here!'

'What do you say? Your father kills me for your sake and you say you will leave this house because I trouble your father. Modisane! matebele a a ntolla – these ndebeles spell bad luck for me. My brother is dead. If he was not dead you two would not speak to me like that. I shall leave this house and go back to my people. They still like me.'

She sobbed like one bereaved: 'Yooo – yooo. Ke bonwa kenang – who sees me?'

Moipone ignored her mother's cries and pleadings and gave her father the food which she had prepared before she left to practise with Mr Samson for the December yearly competition. After a while, when her mother had finished her cryings, she gave her water to wash herself and then gave her food also.

'Moipone, my child,' began her father when he had finished his meal. 'Your mother is like a child,' and he stopped in meditation. 'Your mother should not have answered me when I scolded her for coming late and for not giving you advice on how you should treat Sephai on Wednesday.'

Martha shrugged her shoulders when she heard the name of the person who was to pay her a visit. 'Sephai! What does it mean?' she thought to herself.

'Give me a scale of beer, my child. I must tell you how a man is treated at my home.'

He gulped down half the pint measure and put it on the floor.

'Ndala's child is coming here on Wednesday. He is coming to speak to you and ask you to marry him.' He paused and took another mouthful from the scale. 'Give me some more.'

Martha went down onto her knees and placed the measure in front of her father, wiping the outside.

'You have not done your work thoroughly, my child.'

She looked mystified.

'Look at the measure you have given me, and look at the other dishes in the house.'

There were saucers and plates on the kitchen dresser and it struck Martha that she had not placed the measure on a dish. She took a plate and put the measure upon it.

'Kea leboga Ndebele – I thank Ndebele.'

Martha wondered what her father was going to say next, but instead of telling her how she would treat the visitor, he pulled off his boots and the smell of his feet filled the house. Martha then realized that her father was giving her practical lessons. She took away the shoes and brought a bowl of warm water and, placing it before him, she was about to take soap and a piece of rag to wash his feet, but he said:

'You wash your man's feet, not your father's. You should have washed them when you were still a virgin. And another thing, my child, I cannot show you how you should attend to him in bed.'

His wife raised her head and looked at him and then at her daughter.

'When you have finished giving your man water before and after meals and you notice him wanting to go to bed, you go and arrange the blankets for him, then you can go and goitisa with the other women until such time as you think he needs you.'

The mother and daughter looked at each other, as if to say: 'You go and arrange the bed for him now.'

Martha had seen her mother sometimes kneeling before her father when giving him food, but never doing such things as her father had mentioned. The day her father's cousin had paid a visit, she had seen her father blush when her mother pushed a plate in front of the visitor without going down on her knees, and after meals she did not bring water until Ndala began licking the remains of food from his fingers.

'I shall have a lot of trouble if that boy marries me,' thought Martha.

Mabongo noticed the reaction from his wife when he mentioned the preparation of the bed. He looked at her:

'You are a mother, and a mother is the one to give law to her child if she is a girl. I am forced to say these things to my own child because soon when she is married they will laugh at the Mabongos and say: "They have no law in their home".'

He turned to his daughter, his face serious and grieved. Folding his arms across his chest, he leaned back in the chair – his thin lips showing pale in the dim light that served the one-roomed home.

'I am born of a man who is strict to his wives. If any one of them does not do his law, he sends her to her home to go and get law, and if she still does not carry out what is wanted, he sends her back for the last time and gets his cattle back and all their calves.'

Mathloare and Martha shivered and he noticed that both the mother's and daughter's breasts were trembling against their blouses.

'Is he going to leave his house because I did not do some of the things he has been saying? I have no more people, except my brother at Lady Selbourne and he has taken a woman who does not know her husband's people. Where shall I go?' thought Mathloare.

'Pa!' Martha opened her mouth after a long time, for she had been absorbing all her father had instructed her. 'Pa,' she repeated, 'you frightened us.'

'Don't be afraid, my child. The gods tell me to tell you women's things because your mother does not tell you.'

Mabongo cleared his throat, set his hands on the table and moved the candle nearer his daughter:

'It may not be Sephai who will marry you. It may be someone whom I don't know. Perhaps by then I shall be with my grandmothers in Heaven. When you don't know these laws other women will laugh at you. They will take your man from you and make him happy and you will say he is a bad man and the women are baloi. The doctors will eat your money

64

and say, "We will make him come back". You will wait many moons and will not sleep at night and you will become as thin as a stick of grass. Other men who loved you when you were still fat because your husband made you fat and beautiful, will not come to your house any more. A house without a man is not a home.'

He coughed to clear the lump that was in his throat after his last words. Mathloare looked embarrassed: 'I never cared to know my parents-in-law. Today I look like a fool whilst this man tells my girl child how to behave,' she thought to herself. 'My grandfather also had plenty of wives and they all liked him. In which house did he sleep? I don't know. We went to sleep and left him sitting at the kgotla (the council), and sometimes, when a person went to pass water during the night, he was seen going into one of his wives' houses. But if you rose very early to see where he was you would find him where you had left him the previous night. They used to say that all the women were too many for him and his brothers got into some of the small wives' houses and made children for him. But he was not jealous, he only complained if a child did not look like him.

'Why do I not know what to tell my children when I got them? Today I have one and I only know how to go and look for love medicine. If this meratiso does not work any more the man will leave my child and, as this lethebele says: "laughed at by other women". He knows too much about women.'

'Give me another measure,' Mabongo asked his daughter.

Martha found it a relief to get outside into the fresh air where she had to go to scoop the beer out of a tin hidden from the police. 'It's a bright moonlight night for me and George to take a stroll,' she mused. And as she looked up at the sky she longed to be part of it.

'Blue moon, you saw me standing alone, without a love of my own,' she sang aloud. 'Miss Treswell has complained to Mr Samson that I am not singing so well,' she thought. 'She says my voice has become a little hoarse. She is disappointed that I have deteriorated. It is since all this business with Ndala's child. I was quite happy with George, but he is a crook. He has a lot of girls, in Sophiatown, Newclare, George Gogh – and, who knows, he may already have some in Orlando. But he is afraid of Pimville because the Mashoeshoes will knock him with kerries and if the manyos – Basutho women – try to hide him in their blankets his feet will show that he is a man and not a woman.'

She returned to the house and placed the beer in front of her father in the befitting manner: 'Ndebele.' He thanked her.

'It is night Papa. Soon you must wake up.'

'Yes my child – that lekgoa – white man – does not like the other people to touch the horses.'

'You will sleep beer,' rejoined his wife, 'and then you will refuse to wake up.'

65

'Ah! You, Ma-Moipone, sleep with your head covered and never know whether the sun has risen or it is still night.'

He took a third mouthful and breathed heavily, as if he had been riding a bicycle: 'I have said,' he began to unfold his big indaba, 'that women will laugh at you and you will say they have enticed your man with medicines to love them. But, my child, sehlare only works on sick people and if you are not sick it does not work. The only medicine that works if you are not sick is boloi. If woman gives a man sehlare of boloi, then he dies. A woman who refuses her man the blankets loses him to other women. The other women give him the medicine that his wife does not give him and he likes them and forgets to go to her and she says: "Maseman-mang – mother of so and so – has takata my man. She is a moloi".'

His wife hid her face in shame: 'These are man's things which should not be told to children,' she thought.

'Moipone, go and sleep. You keep your eyes open the whole night like a moloi,' said Martha's mother.

'She has to know these things if she is to be a woman,' protested her father. 'Soon she will be married and she will have children. If she refuses her man with blankets the children will have no father because the man will say: "How can this child be mine when you, mosali, refused me with blankets. Go to the man to whom you gave blankets." And if old people say: "Raage, father of so and so, why do you throw away your children?" He will say: "I don't share with another man."

'Now I have finished my child. On Wednesday Sephai is coming to see you. If you behave like a girl and leave him in the house and run after your marabi man your gods will turn their face away from you. You will be a lekgoba of your mates, for ever, until you go into the earth.'

'I have heard, my father.'

Thereupon Mabongo got straight into bed, which had already been warmed by his wife who had gone to sleep when her husband rebuked her. 'She has got to know these things,' he told himself. He slept soundly.

'Tsoga – wake up – ntate Moipone. The small hand of the clock points at four and the big one at six.'

'Sleep is nice. I am tired of working.'

Whilst he was washing outside Moipone lighted the primus stove and brewed tea. The 'house' where the Mabongo family lived was not more than 15 by 20 feet. In summer the mealies were cooked outside and some of the household goods of little value were kept outside in the yard. Martha had slept in the same room as her parents from babyhood to womanhood and felt little inconvenience, except when she had visitors. She did not complain.

After Mabongo had left for work mother and daughter started discussing the lessons of the previous night.

'Your father cares much about telling you how to treat a man. But he does not care where you treat that man. I must sit here and the mok-goenyana, the son-in-law, sits there,' she said, pointing to a bench opposite her. 'When I am oppressed by air I can't release myself. All these years he has talked about going home and his cousin has also talked about it. Ndala has his children at home and now his first child is working with him, and they say his girl child has finished her lebollo, and she wants to find work in town.'

'Why doesn't he go home? He has a lot of cattle and goats.' Martha stared intently at her mother as she asked this, for she wanted to find out whether the Ndalas had cattle to pay her brideprice.

'Ah! You talk about cattle! Two kraals full! They milk, and give to the pigs. Other people just come and milk some of the cattle for themselves and in exchange for the milk give their children to look after the cattle. They are rich, my child. If he marries you, you won't want to come to town any more.'

'Ma, I still don't understand why Ndala and my father came to work for white people when they have a lot of cattle.'

'My grandfather was also very rich, but he went to Kimberley to work for white people because some white men came to our village and arrested men, young and old, for poll-tax, and my grandfather said he would not sell his cattle to the white man with a white hat, who sat under a monato tree. All the men gathered in the kgotla, and the Chief told them to pay the opgaf or join for the mines so as to get the money to pay opgaf. My grandfather joined and never came back.'

'Ma, I was born in town. I don't know the laws of the people at home and Sephai is not a boy like the town ones. He is what we call "skapie-sheep". He won't allow me to go to the Social Centre or bioscope.'

Her mother sighed: 'My child, marriage is very hard. But Soshal Senta and baiskopo will give you a baby and no father. Home law is nothing: cook nice, give people water before you give them food, go and fetch water from selibeng, keep lapa nice and like people.'

Untying the parcels she had got from the doctor the previous day Martha's mother said, 'I shall give you medicine that will make Sephai like you. This string you tie round your waist when you go out. It will make the men who only want to spoil you run away from you. This one you wear around your neck when Ndala's child comes here tomorrow, and every day that you know you are going to see him. He will not sleep when he thinks of you. But when you wear that one of the waist it will never let any man hold you by the waist. His fingers will shrink and he may even die where he is standing.'

'Ma, it is no good to kill other people.'

'You will see that they don't touch your waist. Keago rapela – I beg you, my child, only until Ndala's child pays cattle for you.'

Sephai was five years older than Martha and his father was satisfied that a man should be older than his wife. He was tall and lean with a light complexion which he had derived from his mother.

'Boesman, staan een kant!' was the order given by the Pass Officer when he had gone to register for work with Mrs McDonald – 'Bushman, stand to one side.' But after it was found that he did not understand a word of Afrikaans he was registered as a 'native'. 'Kaffir-boesman, the Polisie sal jou nooit pas vra nie!' 'Kaffir-bushman, the police will never ask you for your pass,' they told him.

His father often felt ashamed to introduce him as his son.

'Hau! Your child?'

'Yes, he has taken from his mother.'

Having realized that there was some miscegenation, the inquirer left the matter unsolved and accepted the explanation.

The McDonald family treated him with sympathy: 'He might be a descendant of some of my family. God knows the sins of men.' So Mrs McDonald reflected, without revealing her thoughts to her husband.

After finishing the housework by ten o'clock, Sephai went to wash in the toilet-bathroom built for servants. Teddy the McDonalds' son followed him.

'Are you going to bring her here John?' he asked.

'Ja. You tell missus, I hit you. You no tell missus, I take you by bicycle to school. You hear?'

Teddy promised Sephai that if his girl paid him a visit he would keep the secret.

Sephai was a young man who avoided going to the African residential areas for fear of malaitas and other gangsters. On his days off he spent his time at the Zoo Lake with girls and boys from his home, talking about seasonal ploughing and the marriages of some of their older mates.

He knew Doornfontein but not the street. His father had given him the address written on a piece of paper and this he held in his hand and stopped the first person he met in Doornfontein.

'26 Staib Street? Go down this street, pass the next one and then you will come to it.'

Staib Street was devoid of the crowd that gathered on the pavements on Sundays. Little girls played next to the Indian shop and took no notice of the stranger who was approaching them.

'Lemelang – good day. Can you please tell me the house of Moipone?'

'Haaa! Moiponeee. You want ausi Moipone's man to hit her? She is going to be married next month. Grandfather who works in town killed a goat for her. He says he is going to send his child to love Ausi Moipone.'

Tiny dashed into the yard like a paper blown by the wind.

'Ausi Moipone, there's a man – looks like lekgoa. He asks: "Moipone".'

Martha wondered who it could be who looked like a white man who wanted her. She had expected to see a dark complexioned man that looked like 'father' Ndala.

'Call him to come here.'

Martha's heart beat fast and perspiration ran down her face as a young man, led by Tiny, approached. 'This is the boy I have to marry! He looks strong. George will not try to fight with him.'

He walked as if he feared the ground would fall under him. People in the yard stared at him. They were people 'looking at mokgoenyana – bridegroom'.

'He is going to marry Moipone,' he thought these people were saying to one another.

Martha's mother was not at home when the young man arrived. Without a thought Martha left the house and went to sit in the Angle Road entrance to the yard. Tiny led Sephai into the passage and, without knocking, opened the door of the Mabongo home, calling out, 'Ausi Moipone.' Leaving the young man in the room she went to look at the back.

'Assss! Ausi Moipone, now you are afraid of that aubuti and yet you said I must call him in!'

'Tell him I am not in.' she said in a low voice, and Tiny went back to the house giggling and dancing the Charleston, snapping her fingers to the stranger to indicate that the girl he wanted to see was shy to be seen. On noticing that the stranger did not understand her singing and signs she covered her face with both hands and pointed outside.

Fifteen minutes elapsed while the frightened destined lovers put off meeting each other. 'I hope she doesn't come.' He looked at his watch. 'If it strikes two o'clock and she is still not here I shall leave.'

'Tiny, go and watch and see when that aubuti leaves and come and tell me . . . I shall wait for him near the shop and pretend that I see him for the first time.'

Ma-Mapena had heard Tiny speaking to the stranger and wondered what Martha could be doing outside. She went to look.

'You sit here and leave a stranger to sit alone in the house! You have no law. Stand up and go and see him!'

Feeling ashamed Martha complied. She opened the door slightly and peeped inside.

'Tsena – go in.' Tiny pushed her from outside. Although she was heavy and could have resisted, she pretended to stagger, having to support herself on the table in order not to fall. She sat on the bench slightly behind the stranger.

'Lumela.'

The stranger cleared his throat and answered the salutation: 'Ahe.'

The two sat facing each other in silence for five minutes.

'I am a fool,' thought Sephai to himself, 'why don't I speak?' He cleared his throat for the third time and turned his face to the girl.

'Are you Moipone?'

'Yes,' she answered.

He cleared his throat again: 'I have come to see you.' He moved towards her and offered his hand for greeting. He held her hand tightly. She felt powerless to break the grip.

'George is weak. He has tried to hold me like this and I just pulled my hand away easily.'

The two stood looking at each other, wishing no disturbance: they thought of talking and talking the whole night in bed, of people gathering to talk about their marriage, of a little one crying for its mother, while its grandmother took it and put it on her back: 'My grandchild – haa! Where could I have got it from if it was not my child Sephai?'

'I want to speak to you about love. Do you love me?' Sephai had taken a bold resolution not to leave before he had told her that he loved her.

'I don't hate you.' She answered by avoiding the question.

'Kiss me if you don't hate me.'

'I shall kiss you at your place. Not today. When you have given me the address I shall come and then kiss you.'

Sephai let her hand drop. He felt as if he had been knocked with a knobkerrie. He sat down and panted like a bull that has been hoofing the ground in preparation for a fight and then is turned away from its opponent.

A day before the annual concert Martha went to visit Sephai. To look like a woman she dressed in a navy blue skirt, lace blouse which prominently showed her buxom breast, and instead of the badimo necklace she wore a golden chain with a heart locket prominently displayed between her breasts. She completed her dressing with a white headgear tied with a reef knot in front and a bow at the back with a tail running down her shoulders. To prevent her hands from swinging loosely, she held an umbrella thrown over her shoulder and a small handkerchief in the other hand.

It was before noon when she left home. Tiny, who would have hailed her as well-dressed, was at school. She left by the Angle Road gateway to avoid being seen. Along the way she passed a group of road workers.

'Ngelala nge saka – I sleep with sacks.'

'Hallo baby.'

Two or three of the workers left their work and proclaimed their admiration by lying across the road to show that they would die for her. A delivery man alighted, parked his bicycle, and tried to hook her arm to demonstrate how they would walk when they got married.

Martha found the address she wanted without much difficulty. Sephai, who had been on the look-out for her, rushed to the gate and led her into the yard. He unlocked the door of his room and Martha seated herself on a paraffin tin behind the door.

'Come and sit here.' Sephai invited her to sit on the bed which was the only furniture in the room.

'I didn't believe you would come.' Sephai rounded his arm along her

70

waist. His blood thrilled from head to foot as if electrified. His mouth cavity dried and found no moisture for his tongue. His eyes went blank and saw only tiny sparkling things. When his sight returned both were breathing heavily and sat looking at each other like a mouse and cat.

'I love you Moipone. I want you to be my wife and I want a child.'

'Not now,' answered Martha. 'Tonight we will make a child.'

'Not tonight. Now. I can't wait until the sun goes down.'

Teddy had been listening outside. He pushed open the door.

'John, is that your wife?'

Sephai pushed him out: 'Stand outside.'

Mrs McDonald had noticed that Sephai was not in the kitchen. 'John . . . ' she called out. Sephai rushed out of the room and Teddy, who had hurt his knee slightly when pushed from the room, stood by nursing it but showed no ill-feeling when Sephai passed him.

A pile of dishes had been left in the scullery unwashed and flies swarmed about like bees.

'You can't leave dishes like this,' Mrs McDonald screamed at the top of her voice. Sephai began washing the dishes. He took two at a time and both slipped from his shaky hands and smashed on the floor.

'Are you mad, John? My dinner set! A present from my aunt!'

'John has got a girl in his room, Mummy.'

Mrs McDonald rushed to the room and pushed the door open.

'What are you doing in this room? Get out! I will call the police for you.'

As Martha reached the gate Sephai ran through the front door, spoke a few words to her and thrust some coins into her hands. He returned and went straight to his room, covered his face and could be heard weeping.

Mrs McDonald went out to him and, as the door was not closed, she walked to the bed where he was sitting. 'I am sorry John. You should have told me that you had a visitor.' She patted him on the shoulder. 'Don't cry like a child. Teddy is laughing at you. I will give you a day off next week to go and see her.'

Martha was not surprised at being thrown out in this manner by Mrs McDonald. On many occasions her father had told the family how dogs had been set on him for entering the wrong yard on deliveries, and when he explained himself the usual apology was: 'I am sorry my boy. I thought you were a thief.'

6

THE BANTU MEN'S Social Centre was the only entertainment place built exclusively for African men to join. A free bioscope for children showed on Friday nights. It was at these shows that boys in particular learned gangsterism, from such pictures as *Tarzan the Mighty*. They prized Tarzan as a daring man and emulated *Our Gang* to prove that they were town boys.

Boys and girls came to the bioscope from Vrededorp, Doornfontein, Prospect Township, City Suburbs, even as far as Sophiatown. After the bioscope they left a sparkling trail of urine along Eloff Street, making the street their own, until group by group they dwindled from Eloff Street and drifted to the suburbs where they lived.

There were fewer motor cars in the streets those days. The streets were clear of cars by the time late pedestrians went home. The 'bio' goers were free to skate along Eloff Street and along the Main Road to Martindale and Sophiatown.

On a certain Friday night, Charlie Chaplin in *City Lights* was shown. When it was over Mr Phillip, the organizer, switched on the lights and announced to the yelling youngsters that *Rin Tin Tin* would not play. There was going to be a concert. Then there was whistling and pushing to leave.

Gangs stood in groups on the street. A large board advertised

CONCERT AND DANCE
HERE TONIGHT
COME AND HEAR
MISS V. THEMBA
AND
MISS M. MABONGO

Another poster displayed a jazz band, with George shown playing a piano.

'That is George. My child's father. He belongs to my chest. I don't like that Mabongo bitch. He is mine,' a girl dressed in a short tussore pleated skirt was telling a group of boys and girls standing on the pavement opposite the posters. The speaker was Maria, George's other girl who lived in Vrededorp.

'Ons sal sien waar sal hy speel,' responded one of the boys.

A girl yelled: 'Ek sal die bitch steek, Maria. I'll stab the bitch. Aren't I Bitch-Never-Die?'

The Black Cat, the leader of the gang, puffed smoke from a brown rolled paper and a headaching smell caught some of the well-dressed gentlemen and ladies. They coughed and covered their nostrils: 'Kyk wat maak hulle! Look! Dagga!'

At half past eight a shining car made a U-turn at an intersection on Eloff Street Extension and stopped a few feet away from the gang. Men dressed in evening clothes alighted and unloaded musical instruments.

Maria had been dancing and shouting. She stopped and disappointedly said: 'George isn't here yet.'

A second car arrived after a few minutes. George and others unloaded the drums: 'My kind se pa! George belongs to my chest!'

72

George walked to the screaming girl and warned her to stop shouting his name.

'Ja, jy moet jou kind kom vat! Come and fetch your child!' taunted Bitch-Never-Die.

A third car arrived, driven by a white person. Mr and Mrs Samson got out, followed by Martha and Miss Treswell. Martha walked gracefully in the company of cultured people and felt herself one of them. A black woollen shawl was draped across her shoulders.

'Martha, don't look about and shout when greeting people,' Mrs Samson advised her.

'There is that bitch of George's,' snorted Maria.

Bitch-Never-Die continued to sharpen her knife.

The porter escorted Mr Samson's group to some reserved seats and took their cases to the dressing room.

The floor of the Social Centre was already crowded with dancers:

My dog loves your dog,
And your dog loves my dog
And if our doggies love each other why can't we?

Next to the Social Centre a Zulu war dance was in progress. Feet stamped the ground in time to the rhythmic singing and clapping of the men and the dust rose high in the air.

The contrast between the western and the African dance was notable. The one, a shuffling of the feet, and the other, a vigorous stamping. The latter a dance of people witnessed by a large crowd and the other of dancers unwitnessed, men and women locked to each other. The free air swept away the perspiration of the Zulus. The closed air polluted the hall and when the music stopped there was coughing.

Whilst both dances were in progress, the Black Cat gang held a conference in an adjacent yard, about two hundred yards away from the main entrance. The 'Black-Jack' Municipal police did not see them because they sat in the dark, and they could not be heard even if they raised their voices.

'George has left us in the Marabi. He was our player. He has now gone to the teacher.' The Black Cat coughed and puffed dagga from his pipe and passed it over to Bitch-Never-Die.

'My cry to George is that he left me with a small baby. He now loves that Doornfontein girl.' Maria flapped her thighs with her hands.

Bitch-Never-Die looked up at the stars and puffed out long twisted smoke. She appeared to be in deep meditation: 'Ou Bra Black Cat,' she stopped and looked at Maria. 'Ou Bra Black Cat. Jul mors tyd.' She again looked stealthily at Maria: 'You're wasting time, Ou Bra Black Cat. I want George.'

Maria twitched and extended her hand to ask for a smoke.

'Ek wil jou man hê.'

The Chief looked at Maria and laughed: 'Hoor jy, Maria? Bitch-Never-Die wants your man!'

'What do you want to do with George?'

'I want to suck him.'

Maria blushed. Without courtesy she snatched the dagga pipe from Bitch-Never-Die.

'I want George's girl. I like girls who look nice,' said Black Cat.

'Not my man,' said Maria within herself.

'Wat sê jy, Maria? Your man being sucked by Bitch-Never-Die? She is fat. Ou arme George is short. Ou B will suck him to the bone.'

More and more of the Black Cat gang arrived. A messenger had been sent to Vrededorp to tell them that the Social Centre was to be stormed that night, and that the Chief must have a woman.

In the mist of dagga smoke and the tumult caused by the new arrivals, Maria stole away to warn George of the plot they were making to kidnap him.

There was a quick and agitated knock at the door of the Centre.

'Ubani – who is it?'

'Bula, kenna Maria.'

The doorkeeper although he knew that Maria was a member of the Black Cat gang, opened the door. 'What do you want?'

'Please call George for me,' said Maria in a trembling voice.

'Anything gone wrong, Maria?'

'His mother very sick.'

When he heard the message George dashed to the door.

'George, my man, Bitch-Never-Die wants to siep you tonight. A gang has arrived from Vrededorp to catch you.'

George knew Bitch-Never-Die to be reported as a strong woman who could never let a man sleep. She worked in Mayfair. When she resumed her duties in the morning she locked her captive in the room, and unlocked when she desired a dooze from him.

George ran back into the hall and told Mr Samson that the Black Cat gang was going to kidnap Martha. Mr Samson was a strong man who, in his youthful days had never laid down his sticks against an opponent. Before he opened a school of music he had coached boxers, and the Boxing Club boys at the Social Centre were mostly his trainees. He had produced professionals as well as amateurs.

'George, if I was not accompanied by the Europeans I would teach the Black Cat gang a lesson.'

He called Miss Treswell and Martha aside and told them what he had been told by George. Martha blushed and quivered: 'Maria, George's girl, will not last a minute in front of me, and I am not afraid of Bitch-Never-Die.' She meditated to herself, 'if she is a bull-fighter, she will meet another bull-fighter.'

She looked at George: 'Men like George are pap, soft like porridge.'

She thought of her father, still respected by the Malaitas as their king. 'My father would bleed everybody in this hall.' Her father had told stories of his fights at Marabastad, of Sergeant Van Rooyen begging him to stop fighting, of the pick-up van escorting his boys to Brooklyn.

George urged Martha to get ready to leave: 'There is no time to waste. I have been told that the gang is arranging men to break doors and windows.'

He led her by the hand through the members' door, escorted by members of the Boxing Boys Club. Maria had rejoined the Black Cat gang which was still in conference in the nearby field.

A taxi, with Martha and George sitting in the back seat, accelerated. 'Sofifi-toe, driver.'

'George, jy kan nie vir my so treat.'

'You take orders from me, driver. She is my wife. She must go where I order her to go. Kaman driver, speed!'

The dance in the hall continued.

'The nights are long without you my Russian sweetheart.'

The war dance outside had stopped and the dancers now tossed on their bunk beds and dreamt about their song at work:

'Umlungu ko-dam – Whiteman be damned.'

The Black Cat gang was a Vrededorp gang. Maria lived in Vrededorp and Bitch-Never-Die worked nearby in the European suburb.

Black Cat, the leader of the gang, was a miscegenation of Coloured and African. He could speak neither Sesuthu, which was his father's language, nor Afrikaans, his mother's language, well. He could not finish a sentence in a single language.

'Is die mosali wil nie moet die monna bly, een moet vir sy moet matla bly wat – if a woman does not want to stay with a man one must force her.'

The residents of Vrededorp were mixed as the league of nations: Malay, Coloured. Indians, Africans, Afrikaners and English, separated by no-mans open ground. There were even a few Damaras. The children all played together and understood each other.

The Black Cat gang had learned the techniques of gangsterism at the free 'bio' operated by the Bantu Men's Social Centre. Black Cat had admired the 'Mystery Man'. But he had preferred to call himself the Black Cat because of his black and penetrating eyes.

When he was younger he had been arrested and kept at Auckland Park Juvenile Detention Camp. There he had met other gangsters from Pimville. In the evenings Bra Thabo of Pimville had confessed how he had raped a girl at a lonely spot in Kliptown. Impressed by this bravado the Black Cat was encouraged to confess to the police to his own charges. So the mind of the Black Cat became steeled and he cared not for arrest.

Nearly half-an-hour had elapsed since Maria's return to the gang conference and she reckoned that George must have left the hall: 'Ou Bra Black Cat, jul mors tyd. Get the boys ready to invade the hall.'

The boys, led by Black Cat, banged the door: 'Maak julle oop. Open up. Ek is Black Cat.'

They kicked the door and laughed and Maria and Bitch-Never-Die screamed.

'Ons het die bitch vanaand – we've got the bitch tonight.' They laughed as if they were enjoying the film of Charlie Chaplin in *City Lights*.

Inside the hall the band continued to play. The Boxing Club boys took their pre-determined positions in the hall. The women were led out of the fire-escape door. The band went on playing.

Suddenly the door burst open and in rushed the gang. Maria and Bitch-Never-Die raised their voices in discordant song: 'Tjeka, tjeka messie.' They shouted and grabbed any man: 'Dans met my. Dance with me. Laat staan die bly meid. Ek is jou vrou.'

The hall was half empty. The door had been shut when only half the gang was inside. The lights went off. There was wailing from different parts of the hall. A cry of 'Yoooooo - yoooooo, me yoooooo. A se naa – it's not me.' Then came a cry of 'Help me men! Bitch-Never-Die has hold of me underneath.'

'Die boys van Black Cat fight to the last man,' came the command.

The door was being hammered from the outside. A police whistle, a rushing of heavy boots, then a command outside: 'Vang hulle, die black sams. Bamba. Catch them.' A police whistle, far down Eloff Street. And a youthful voice: 'Ntate, it is not me. It's Black Cat.'

Again there was a banging on the door from outside: 'Vula. Poyisa.'

The lights flashed on in the hall and on all sides were injured gang members and Boxing Club boys. The floor was bloodstained. Bitch-Never-Die stood in a corner panting like a bull-frog. The harsh light showed up the ugly scars on her face. She was snorting and puffing, ready for another fight. The Black Cat lay groaning like an injured tiger in a corner.

'He is seriously injured,' said a policeman.

Maria had slipped through on to the platform. She sat in a corner, looking like a terrified owl. The Black Cat was carried out to an ambulance – his lips as pale as winter grass, his head moving from side to side. He had no stab wounds but seemed to have been punched all over his face and kicked in the ribs and face. A policeman had to put up a tough fight to arrest Bitch-Never-Die. She flung herself at him and sunk her teeth deep into his flesh.

The car in which Martha and George were travelling drove at normal speed along Eloff Street into Market Street, westward, and then to Bree Street at the Market, going under the bridge on the way to Vrededorp. The streets were poorly lit. The shop windows were dark. There were no night-watchmen. Not a soul was in sight. The upstairs windows of one house were open and a single curtain flagged the room, which seemed to be without occupants. Even a burglar would have feared to break in – human beings fear a quiet house as much as they fear to pass a graveyard during the night. A few yards further on there was a row of closely built slum-like cottages. Each cottage could not have had more than three rooms, bathroom and pantry excluded. All the windows were tightly shut. A cry of a baby could be heard from inside one house and the lights of the car showed a white woman soothing the baby. No electric light bulb dangled on the verandah. The two steps led directly into the street.

The driver drove cautiously and dimmed the lights. They passed a graveyard. On the far side of the graveyard a glowing fire was burning and it lit up the tomb-stones.

'Is that a spook?' inquired Martha.

George wiped his brow and breathed heavily. But the driver had driven many a time in the night. Two months ago he had taken part in a shop-breaking in the centre of the city. The glowing fire had been burning then too, but no ghost had stopped him.

On the left of the road stood the Bridgman Memorial Nursing Home. A night watchman stood in the main entrance, checking on a taxi carrying an expectant mother. Martha caught the cries of babies: 'Oh my Lord. George is driving me to have a baby!' She pictured herself sleeping next to a baby in that nursing home.

'Turn to your right and stop after you have crossed three streets. There is a big house in front there. Stop there.'

The house where the car stopped appeared to be an old mansion: dilapidated window curtains, panes hanging loosely, a twisted iron sheet threateningly dangled in front of the door. The cement pillars still held the roof, and fastened to one of the pillars was a black painted board: 'Night Club Boys.'

'Stop driver. This is the Cavern.' George unleashed a key from his trouser pocket and unlocked the door which creaked as if begging for mercy not to be pushed too hard. He used his shoulder to get it open. Martha entered after him, after being threatened that if she remained outside the 'Thota Ranch' would take her. 'Die is Sophiatown – it's not Doornfontein: the Thota Ranch don't play games.'

The mansion consisted of about eight rooms, occupied by as many families. In the yard behind there were also rooms, more than in the mansion, and as it was a weekend a number of the occupants were still awake, the 'aunties' serving their customers.

'The children want to sleep. Please go.' An 'auntie' was heard pleading with a customer who pretended to be asleep. And in another house there was a concert of drunkards, each singing his own tune. A cloud of smoke gave the yard the appearance of a furnace workshop and its fumes choked the husband of a woman who was selling to customers. He coughed and spat on the floor and fell again to snoring. The 'auntie' being a young woman, attractive and talkative, spoke to a well-dressed man, who said his farewells several times and then sat again to demand a nip of brandy and pour a glassful for the woman to drink. He asked the woman to sit next to him, and when she sat he put his arm around her hips and patted them. The sleeping man coughed again, as if warning the two that he was watching them.

'Pas op hy sien vir ons, Look out,' she said. The man stood up again and bade her goodnight and stood at the door waving at her to come outside.

George and Martha had entered a dark room and George searched for matches without avail: 'Wait, I shall go to that house for matches,' he said, after trying to force Martha to lie down without light.

On seeing George approach, the well-dressed man left the woman he had been holding in his arms and pressing against himself and fled out of the yard.

There were two beds in the room, each covered with clean blankets and linen cloths which served as sheets. In one corner there were unwashed pots with white foam lapping over the edges. A copper coloured object that looked like a primus stove lay among the heap of dishes and pots.

'George, you are a blue-nine. A man who really loves his wife would not steal her this way. You crooked Mr Samson by telling him that there was a gang to take me away by force and yet you meant yourself. You are no better than Tarzan the Mighty gang and the Thota Ranch.' Martha wept and turned to look in George's face: 'This is your trade. You have girls all over Johannesburg and in the kitchens. Your children cry all over. God will punish you for that.'

'Martha! You and I have been in love since our school-days. I have been trying to make children by you and I couldn't. I want to make children with you so I have proof that you are a woman. We Zulus don't just take a woman before we know that she can get children. How can my father's cattle go for nothing? A woman must bear children to return the cattle the man has paid for her.' George held her by her fingers. 'Please honey let's sleep,' he said in English.

'Blow the light first,' pleaded Martha who was preparing to undress.

George felt a piece of string around Martha's waist. She pushed his hands lightly from it: 'Don't touch me on the waist. It is against our custom that a man touches a woman on the hips.'

George smelt the animal fat and sneezed. He pushed his hand forcefully back and ripped the string off: 'I don't care for native custom. You are my woman. Tonight you are going to get me a child.'

That night she entered into the life of motherhood. Sleepless nights with the child crying. Sick baby to the clinic. Tender love of motherhood. Battle to bring up a respectful child. Problem of giving it a good education. Its future in a country where a person is not judged according to his talent but by his colour, denied the right to take part in the administration of the country and the right to do skilled work.

On this particular Saturday night Martha conceived a child who, among millions of others, was to spend his life in and out of jail.

'You have no proof that you were born in Sophiatown. Do you know the first Chinaman who ran Fah-fee in Sophiatown?'

'You say your grandfather was a Ndebele. Then your home is Potgietersrust. You must leave the urban area of Johannesburg within seventy-two hours.'

Martha, and many of her time, hoped that the law would treat them as human beings because they had attained a certain measure of civilization. It was not to be. But Martha did not curse her 'sin' when she became pregnant. 'This child is going to work for me.'

The driver came to fetch the couple the next morning. Martha was dropped a street away from her home. She was tired and looked depressed. Her father was not at home but her mother greeted her: 'You look tired Moipone. Singing the whole night is too much. But five pounds is a lot of money. You are not tired for nothing.'

George had thrust five pounds into her hand when she alighted from the taxi: 'Tell your mother that you got third prize.'

The days rolled by, the weeks mounted. No periodical menstruation occurred to Martha. She felt giddy. Food had an unusual smell. She had exquisite sleepiness, hatred for certain people and a deep longing for George, but when she saw him she felt a pang of hatred.

'You are getting a big woman, my child,' said her mother proudly. She was then entering the second month of her pregnancy. 'Your father, Ndala, will be surprised to see you.' Martha grinned but her heart heaved in case her mother would say, 'You are pregnant.'

Mathloare looked at her daughter and scanned her face and became suspicious of her: 'I shall see in the coming months,' she thought to herself.

'I shall go and see Sephai during the week. I want him to find me a job in the kitchens.' Martha's voice shook as she said these words.

'Moipone, you have never been so depressed. You seem to be eaten by something since you went to that marabi concert. Tell me what eats you?'

'Nothing ma. Only worried about work.'

'You make money from your singing. Why do you worry?'

'A woman can't live by singing and leave children alone at night. I must find work.'

'Now you speak like a woman, my child. I told you a long time ago that marabi is for women who don't care to live with men, and don't want to have children. When they get children they kill them at birth and go again to Marabi and look like girls who have never had children.'

79

Martha's face blushed and she looked down at the floor. 'I must go away from this house before they see me.'

She lost interest in singing and stopped going to Mr Samson's house. Miss Treswell, who had undertaken to further her singing career by raising funds to send her abroad, expressed her disappointment to Mr Samson:

'She could be one of the finest singers in the world. But she is just one of the many African children who begin their schooling at a late age, spending wasteful time playing in the streets, without their parents' care. Martha has the talent of a genius. It is a shame that gift should now be spent in scrubbing floors and washing dishes.'

Martha added two more bundles to the washing. The daughter and the mother washed from sunrise to sunset without a break and started ironing after Mabongo had left for work at three o'clock in the morning.

She asked her mother to stop brewing beer for sale: 'Ma, we can help father by doing washing. I can't stand men coming into the house to buy beer.'

When they had managed to convince the customers that they were no longer selling beer, Martha found space to lie down and rest. 'Your man will not stand a lazy woman,' her mother told her.

One day, on her way home from delivering washing, Martha spotted the car that had transported her and George to and from Sophiatown. She hailed the driver.

'Ah! ke wena Martha. I am pleased to see you. I have been with George. He is working for the buses. He is a clerk. He gets a lot of money. He will come and pay lobola for you. You will be rich now.'

'George is not a man who can keep one woman because he has got many hearts. He has got women all over. He sleeps with this one tonight and tomorrow with another one and the day after again with another one and the day after again with a different one,' said Martha.

'He told me that of all these women he likes you the best. He says that you look like a woman. Like a mfundisi woman. He says he wants a woman who will be respected by other women.'

Martha laughed and looked at the print skirt she was wearing. She pulled the black shawl down slightly from her shoulders and kept her hands on its ends.

'Tell him I want to see him very badly. I can't sleep when I think of him. I feel like crying. Bluff him that you saw me walking with another man. He will not waste time to come.'

Sephai had seen Martha several times at her home since the concert and each time he had suggested that she pay him a visit at work. But she declined, saying that his madam was rude: 'I mix with white people. What is your madam? Nothing. I shall come to you when you work for white people who are not rubbish.'

'My missus said that if you come again I must tell her.'

'And then let her boy push the door open and run and tell her that a kaffir girl is in the room? I am sorry, my dear,' she said in English.

'Sephai,' she resumed after a few moments of silence, 'I want you to marry and take me to your home. I want a man who will give my parents cattle and take me to church. I want to wear the nkitsing earrings worn by married women.'

'I have a lot of cattle. I can marry you tomorrow. What is a church? The teacher can't give food when your children are hungry. He only wants money, and eggs when the men have gone to work. I will work for you and you need never come to town any more. You will only look after my children and see that my young brother milks the cows for the children.'

'Then you must send your people to come and ask for me. After that I shall come to your missus' house with cheek and sleep there.'

'My father said he is going to write to my mother to send some women to come and ask for you. They are waiting for the mealies to be reaped.'

'Why can't they come now?'

'The birds will eat the mabele.'

Martha was abrupt in her farewell. Sephai was sad and disappointed.

'Town children are no good. She doesn't know that if you leave mabele in the field the birds will eat it. She thinks it is like washing white people's clothing. At home a woman works hard and chases the birds away the whole day. The sun beats her until she is as black as the soil. They don't play at home. I am going to marry her and she will see that it's not easy to live on the farms.'

George had been arrested for vagrancy under section 17. He had appeared before the Magistrate. He explained that he was making a living by being a bandmaster.

'Your band is not registered. This court cannot consider it a lawful employer. You are therefore warned to find suitable work. You are discharged.'

From there he had explored all places of employment. A bus company where he was known by many employees as a man without any 'politics' gave him a clerical job. He now found very little time to 'check' his girls. But there was some instinct that reminded him of Martha.

'My heart gets a fright when I think of Martha,' he told his close friends.

'I think you have done a damage to her. You better make ready for napkins, boy.' They all laughed and patted him on the shoulders. 'Boy, boy, you are a man. Shake hands.'

When he received the message from his taxi friend that Martha wanted to see him his heart beat against his shirt and his friend could see his discomfort. 'She is not pregnant, boy. Don't get scared. She was walking with another guy. You better go and check up.'

George finished his shift late in the afternoon. He went home, which was not very far from his place of work, to change into private clothes. It was dark when he reached Doornfontein and only a dim light on the corner, the shop light, and an open burning brazier of a watchman at the engineering firm opposite the Molefe yard showed him where he was. George was thankful that it was such a night: 'No-one will see who I am.'

He blew the known whistle, and after waiting a few moments repeated it, this time with a musical ending. Martha had recognized the first sound, and in order to get out of the house she busied herself outside.

George was standing far from the light.

'George,' she called. 'Come here.'

Martha was standing near the shop. 'I don't care if anybody sees us here. I have been long a girl. That time has passed.'

She fixed her eyes on George's face and said: 'You are a nice man. You steal me from the concert and take me to your Cavern and give me five pounds for all the trouble you have made for me. Your five pounds will not even pay for Bridgman Nursing Home.'

'What do you mean?' asked George. 'Do you say I want to nurse at Bridgman Nursing Home?'

'George, don't make yourself a fool. You have a lot of children. You have taken all your wives to Bridgman Hospital. You know what they pay. Maria was the last one. You must take me also to Bridgman.'

Tiny had been hiding in the shop during this discourse and had heard them.

'Yoo! Ausi Moipone is going to get a child. Two men.' She counted them on her little fingers. 'The white one has cattle and this one nothing. He plays marabi. In the night he will leave Ausi Moipone with the children and go to Marabi.'

Bhoola, the shopkeeper, was pounding a red powder in the kitchen and had not seen Tiny behind the door. He came in on his toes and picked her up by the ears and twisted them: 'Bhen-chud. Go out shop!'

She ran out of the shop laughing. Martha caught her by the arm: 'What have you been doing in the shop? If you tell them at home I am going to beat you.'

'Hau! Hau! Ausi Moipone I have not heard anything. Bathong! Ausi Moipone you say I heard something. Not me. I only hid myself in the shop to surprise you.'

The time was 9.30 p.m. The policeman on beat passed and gave a warning glance at the couple. Bhoola, the shopkeeper, prepared to close the shop.

'I have no special pass,' said George.

'When you stole me that night you never cared about a special pass,' retorted Martha.

The policeman passed again: 'If we still find you here next time we will arrest you for nag-pas.'

The shopkeeper closed his shop and retired to the back where his wife and children and father slept.

'I must go,' said George.

'You are my man and I your woman. We slept in Sophiatown as man and woman. We must be arrested together.'

Tiny had gone home and did not tell anybody that Martha was standing outside the shop. Mabongo arrived from work after nine o'clock. At 9.30 he began to be anxious about his daughter's absence from home.

'She has started attending marabis again. I shall go out and look for her.'

Tiny overhead this, and, fearing that he would find Martha and George, she stole out of the house: 'Ausi Moipone, uncle is coming to look for you.' She grasped Martha by the hand: 'He has got sjambok. Let's go, Ausi Moipone.'

'I want to see you tomorrow,' said Martha as George moved away.

George had spent some days and nights in prison after he had been arrested for vagrancy. He had slept on the hard cement with dirty, smelling, infested blankets. Most of the time he had been locked indoors with the other prisoners. The convicted prisoners at the place where the vagrants had been taken after their first appearance before the Magistrate, ill-treated them. The warders pretended not to see. George was forced to give his watch to a long-time prisoner: 'You come to eat food for nothing here. What is a pass? You must be arrested for big things.' Prisoners, who seemed to have made the place their permanent home, boasted of their crimes.

Since he did not want to repeat the experience, George avoided taking streets which were frequented by the police, after leaving Martha, and, when he spotted them, he hid behind buildings and came out after they had passed.

'I am paying for the Sophiatown sleep. She says she is spoiled and that girl is not pap like other girls I have spoiled. She is going to get me into trouble. Mr Samson is very clever. He will help her. I must ask the firm to transfer me to another place,' George thought whilst he dodged the police and ultimately reached his Cavern. He no longer lived with his mother. He spent a sleepless night, tossing from side to side – 'I am going to ask for transfer.' Then a snappy doze overtook him, a nightmare in which he was facing the Native Commissioner. He jumped from the bed, his body swamped in sweat. The morning came as a relief to a mind tormented by terrifying images.

George's shift fell late in the day. He slept soundly through the morning, making up for wasted sleep, and went to work feeling well. He had already gained the confidence of the clerical staff manager. He was competent in his work and rarely late for duties. 'George would be my first preference if it came to promotion,' the staff manager had told his seniors, and so George did not find it too difficult to find the courage to approach him about the matter which had tormented him the whole night: 'If he refuses

I shall have to leave Johannesburg before Martha makes things worse for us.'

He knocked on the door of the manager's office: 'Baas, I want to speak to you, sir.'

'Yes George, what's the matter? Do you want an early off-duty to prepare for Marabi Dance?'

'No sir, I want to speak about transference. I am tired of Johannesburg. My parents have gone to Natal and I want to go and work near home.'

The manager was quiet for some time and George was kept on his feet all the while.

'Come back. I shall call for you.'

He got back to his desk, contemplating the verdict the manager would pronounce. 'I have made up my mind to go. Come what may. I must go.'

The bell rang and he knew he was going to get an answer:

'Two, three, five minutes I shall know the answer.'

'The Company needs experienced clerks for our Durban depot. But you, George, have not yet acquired the necessary experience. I shall, however, send you with two others who will have no difficulty in getting registered in Durban. Stanley and Wellis are Zulus and you are also a Zulu.'

The manager went to the files and took out a document: 'Our new plan for Durban is to start in two months. In the meantime you are to work here. Your name will be forwarded to the Board of Directors for approval.'

'Thank you sir, thank you very much baas.' He left the office backwards, saluting the manager twice.

'It was last month when I took her to Sophiatown. This is the second month. Two more months will be four. I shall give her money and go to her every time. I will not tell anybody that I am going to Durban.'

Ndala went home for a short while to discuss with his wife the prospect of his son getting married to Mabongo's daughter.

'Sephai is your child,' she cried. 'You can get him married where you like. But tomorrow don't cry.'

'We want to get my cousin back home. And we can only make my uncle forgive him by getting his child married to one of us,' he told her.

'Location children don't know home work. They cannot go to the fields or chase birds away. They don't know how to smear the lapa with dung or keep it well. They can't balance a water can on their head.'

'Women learn very quick if they like their parents-in-law. She will also learn.'

Ndala and his wife finally agreed that some women would go and propose a marriage after the reaping.

May, June, July: the reaping season had come. The trading store in the village came to life. Mealies were exchanged for tea and sugar, for meat, for yards of cotton materials, for hard cloth skirts, for khaki trousers.

84

The women who did the exchange received a loaf of bread and a full one-pound packet of sugar poured into a bowl of water. Each snatched as big a piece of bread as she could get and dunked it into the sugared water, eating contentedly: 'We are eating our strength.'

Ndala's wife consulted with her young sister about the journey to town to look for a woman for Sephai. She consented without a word because she wanted to see 'Jubek' (Johannesburg), and a cousin was asked to accompany her.

Ndala, now no more only a cousin to Mabongo but a mokgotse, an intimate friend, advised them that he would be sending some people to look for a woman for his child. They had finished reaping. They would no longer be afraid to leave the fields to the cattle.

George kept up his constant visits to Martha and gave her some money. 'I like my child,' and he would run his hand over Martha's abdomen.

'George, I love you too much but I know you will not marry me. You already have a lot of children. You didn't marry their mothers. How can you marry me?' And she would gently remove his hand.

'It is not me that spoiled Maria. She only blamed me because I was taking her out. At the Native Commissioner she agreed that I was not the only one. The Native Commissioner said he could not find me guilty, because the girl did not know the exact person who had spoiled her.'

'But Maria tells everyone that you are the father of her child,' insisted Martha.

'She is mad. When she sees me, she says it's me. When she sees Richard, she says it's him. Every man who was in love with her is her child's father.'

George never talked about marriage: 'I must first see before I know what I am doing.' That was the only answer he would give Martha when she inquired about marriage.

After these visits Martha would come home late, but before her father returned from work.

'Oh my child, you have started coming late. You will spoil your marriage. The people are coming to look for you next moon.' Her mother passionately expressed her fears that these late-hour visits would be noticed by jealous people who would tell her bakhotse that the girl was no good.

The bus company received an urgent message from Durban that there was a shortage of staff due to some men enlisting in the army. Drivers, conductors and clerks were urgently needed.

'George,' called the clerical staff Manager, 'go and pack up your luggage. You are leaving by transport tonight for Durban.'

He ran out of the office like a whirlwind to his home.

'Auntie, you can have the pots. Jy, Sonny, you have the bed. I want the bicycle because I want to see Durban every day.'

'Yoo, buthi George. Who is going to play at the African Hall?' A group of children clustered around him.

Young and old shook hands with him: 'Hamba kahle. Sizo buya si bonane – we will see each other again.'

Two women alighted at Jeppe Station and asked a pedestrian where Doornfontein was. It was the day after George had left for Durban. The times of arrival were almost the same – in the morning between nine and ten o'clock.

The shorter distance travelled by the women in the train had been tiresome and slow. The long distance travelled by George and the bus group was boring but quick. George had escaped from Martha. The women had come to seek marriage for their 'son'.

George and the bus crew plunged immediately into work after their arrival in Durban. Martha sent a note to the Johannesburg bus depot saying: 'Dear George, don't come tonight.' And the visitors sat dead tired in a house in Sivewright Avenue and waited patiently while the news of their arrival was carried to the bride-to-be.

Meanwhile, in Durban, George was engaged in the tiresome work of learning the routes to the various townships. After work he went to the beer halls to quench his thirst: 'The place is very hot, a man must drink just a mugful.'

He passed among Indian women selling bananas and curry balls. Rickshas were touting for visitors to the sea beach: 'Come in,' one ricksha puller said to two men speaking Afrikaans.

'Hoor wat hy sê. Hy sê "come in". Listen to him!' They laughed and passed.

George scanned and could not believe his eyes. He stopped and stared at the woman coming towards him: 'Ah! Ma-Ndlovu. How did she come to this place?'

'Do I see George or Tokoloshe? Hau! Hau! George uphumaphi – where do you come from?'

Ma-Ndlovu told George that after being robbed by Reverend Ndlovu she went to work. 'I was fed up with the gold city, Igoli, so I came here. Tandi is a big woman, George, you can marry her. She helps me to sell seshimayane beer. I am very pleased to see you. I hold ndudumas on Saturdays and Sundays. You can come and play. Tandi will take care of you. Didn't you marry that fat girl of yours? The one who used to sit near you when you played piano?'

George told her how he had come to Durban but ignored her questions about Martha.

Ndala's younger brother had ordered the herd-boys to delay the cattle in the kraal until he came. Then he selected seven cows.

'Take them out.'

He went about the oxen post.

'Drive these three out.'

86

Then he went to the goat and sheep kraal and, without selecting, drove eight of them out. He took all the animals to July's father.

'Malome, this is the bogadi for your grandchild. You can keep them in your kraal or I shall build a kraal for them until your child comes for them.'

According to African custom and tradition the man's parents do not arrive at the girl's home when wishing to talk about marriage. Another home is selected by the bakgotsis, as they call each other, and the hostess becomes the maditsela – one who takes errands. She would be present at the indaba of the bakgotsis and be the mouth and ears of the visitors and become responsible for Martha's future welfare.

Ndala came to see the visitors after work at the house selected for them by the Mabongos.

'We have sent a word to them that the visitors are here. They have received the message. We have told them that we will see them on Sunday when the father of the girl is here. They have agreed,' he was told.

'Have you seen your ngoetsi?' Ndala asked his sister-in-law.

'I have seen her at the shop, but when she saw me she turned hurriedly into the yard. She is a big woman, like your sister Sarai. This is the right woman for a man. Not a thin woman like a reed. My sister will be very satisfied.'

On Saturday night Mabongo and his wife and the old Mapenas held a talk.

'We shall ask for bogadi as soon as they have asked for mosali.'

'I don't care about church,' rejoined Mabongo when his wife suggested that a Minister be found to officiate at the marriage. 'They only want money. Lobola marriage is better because you get something for your child.'

'Go lokile ntate Moipone – it's all right. You are the man. If you don't want moruti I have nothing to say. The child is yours.'

The night seemed to last for weeks. Both parties kept sleeping a few moments and then waking and saying something about the next morning's affair.

At ten o'clock a message was sent to the Molefe Yard that the visitors were coming.

'Moipone,' said her mother, 'you have to tell the truth. Whether you like the man or not. Tell me now.'

Martha bowed her head and was silent.

'I am speaking to you.'

'What can I say? You like him. I have only to do what you tell me.'

Mr Ndala's sister-in-law was tall and slim and was wearing a short-sleeved blue and white German print cotton frock with a pink calico gown thrown across her shoulders. Her head-dress was of yellow calico coiled and tied in a reef-knot with the ends hanging down behind. A colourful necklace reposed on her robust breast and on her plump arms she wore Union Jack coloured bracelets. She was barefoot.

The other woman, though an Ndebele, had adopted a Tswana form of dress. She wore a spotted German print cotton skirt fringed at the hem with a pink trimming, a cream embroidered blouse and a heavily starched black apron. Her blouse sleeves were long and buttoned. Her head-dress was of silk, tied with a reef-knot on her forehead. She had thrown a light shawl across her shoulders and wore brown shoes.

Accompanied by the maditsela, the two country-women advanced into the yard.

'They've come to seek Mrs Mabongo's daughter, Moipone,' remarked a curious onlooker.

'She's lucky to have her child married,' added another.

Tiny ran to the back of the yard where Martha was occupied with some housework.

'They've come, Ausi Moipone.'

'Who, Tiny?'

'The people are coming to marry you.'

Martha left the work she was doing and breathed to herself: 'Today is today.' She thought of George: 'A crook.' She imagined Sephai: 'Faithful.' But. . . .

The visitors entered the dingy passage and at the first door on the right they stood. 'Ko-ko,' announced the maditsela.

'Tsenang.' Mathloare Mabongo stood to receive the strangers without shaking hands. The atmosphere became stiff as the newcomers greeted: 'Dumellang.' Then they seated themselves on home-made mats opposite Mrs Mabongo, Mrs Mapena and a young woman who was Martha's intimate friend. The maditsela began to chat with Mathloare as if nothing special was happening.

It was according to custom that no men were present at this stage. Ndala's sister-in-law held the status of a mother to Sephai and a future mother-in-law to Martha. She wielded much power to accept or reject the marriage proposals. The other woman, Ndala's aunt's daughter, was to Ndala a 'wife' by virtue of being a cousin. Although she was less influential in the indaba, she wielded a power on behalf of Ndala. She was a source of inspiration or discouragement.

As it was proper to clarify any misunderstanding of the status of each person present, Mrs Mapena asked, 'Le bomang?'

'I am the mouth and the ears of these two women,' replied the maditsela.

'Le tsoa kae?'

'We come from Molethlane. On my right is Ndala's wife's younger sister, and on my left is his cousin.' The introduced women smiled and shook hands, then forestalled the big indaba with idle talk.

'We come from far. Our feet are pricked by the thorns.'

'We give birth to be troubled by the children. They take us to people we don't know.'

The maditsela raised her face. 'We have been sent to the home of Mabongo. Is this the house?'

'Le fithlale teng. You've arrived in it,' declared Mrs Mapena.

Ndala's sister-in-law took a snuff box and emptied a little on to her palm and offered some to her friend.

'We have come,' she began her mission, 'to ask for a bowl of water. We have been sent by our child because he has seen a woman in your kraal and he would like to marry that woman.'

'We have only one bowl of water. We don't want to lose it,' answered Mrs Mapena.

'We know that you only have one bowl. When a person marries from a house where there is only one child he knows that he marries the parents of the woman. He looks after them just as he looks after his own parents.'

Mathloare said: 'If you take away my only child I shall go hungry.' She looked down and scratched the floor with the stick she held all the time.

'We have to call Moipone,' declared the old woman. 'She must answer if she knows these people. We can't say before we hear from her mouth.'

While they waited for Martha, her mother sat tense and inattentive. She visualized men far away, where these women came from, in heavy over-coats and with sticks across their shoulders, looking very tired, coming together to decide how many cattle they would give for bogadi.

There was a stir when Martha entered the room. The two visitors admired her copper colouring and the way she held her body. 'This is a woman who will walk with authority among other women.' She moved with calm and self-possession as at the concerts at the Bantu Men's Social Centre. Miss Treswell had taught her manners complex to the unsophisti-cated women who were discussing her.

'She has no tsabo,' reflected her mother, thinking of the awe expected from a courted girl.

'The fields will squeeze out all her "missus".' thought Ndala's sister-in-law, but she liked the girl in spite of her missus manners. She was not of a different tribe. Only town had made her like this.

'It should have been my brother marrying this girl,' thought Ndala's cousin. She would not be ashamed to go to church with her. 'The white barutis like people dressed like this.'

Martha sat down next to her grandmother, her one hand on the floor, the other holding a honey-comb shawl she wore in respect.

'Moipone,' began Mrs Mapena.

'Ko-koo, grandmother,' Martha responded in her baritone voice.

'Such a voice!' thought Ndala's cousin. 'I've heard of it.'

Mrs Mapena continued: 'These people have come to look for you. They say you told their child to come and look for you here. Now you must tell us if you know them.'

All eyes turned to Martha. Her mother stopped scratching the floor. Ndala's sister-in-law took another sneeze of snuff, but held it between her fingers without offering any to her friend.

There was a long silence as if the minister was preparing the Holy Communion behind the pulpit.

'Moipone, we are talking to you!'

'I don't know them,' Martha answered in a firm voice. Its sound droned deep into everyone's ears. No one could have said 'I have not heard'.

There was a long silence again. The women looked at each other uneasily, not knowing what to say. Mathloare applied the match-stick to her ears. She dug and dug and produced nothing from them. Then Ndala's sister-in-law drew a deep breath and blew it out as if she had been suffocating.

'You have played us fools. We have left our corn in the fields. My brother's mother has selected some cattle for magadi for nothing. My friends, let's go.'

'Mosali,' appealed the old woman. 'You have no patience. You should understand that people can change their minds every now and then. My child, Moipone, must not be understanding what is meant by: 'Wa ba tseba – do you know them?'

She turned to the young woman, to whom she said: 'Take Moipone with you and go and speak with her.'

The young woman was about five years older than Martha. She had been married and had taken part in many marriage ceremonies. She and Martha confided secrets to each other. Now she rebuked Martha: 'Moipone, you have shocked these people. You say you don't know them. What they mean is: "Do you love their boy; do you want to be married by him?" '

'I understand all that they are saying. I told my mother that if they like him I can't stop them. But they can give him a woman they like, not me. I have chosen a man I like.' Then she paused and lifted her hand to stop her friend from speaking: 'Wait, I still want to tell you something. I don't want to put a load on a person who is not the owner.'

'What do you mean?'

'You are a woman and I am a woman. You don't like to say a man is the father of your child when you know that another man is the father. It will eat you and you will get thinner and thinner until everybody says: "She has made a sin".'

'Do you mean to say you are in body?'

'I am a woman. Why should I not get in body? Some girls smaller than me have children. I don't care if I get a child without a father. It is my child. God has willed that I should get it.'

'Moipone, you are a woman. A woman never likes to give someone a thing which does not belong to him. She is proud to say "my child's father, so and so". Who got you into body?'

'Ag! He is just a Marabi boy. He has got a lot of girls. Plenty children. But I love him. He is clever, he is not a skapie like Sephai. I don't like farm boys. They work in the kitchens, take out night chamber pots for the white women and wash their bloomers.'

Martha did not return to where the talk was held. She left for an unknown place.

'Tell us what she said,' Ma-Mapena asked the young woman.

The young woman called her aside: 'She is in body'

Ma-Mapena threw up her hands: 'It is finished! It will not help us to talk. She has been eaten by night animals. People of God, go back to your homes.'

They all understood. They felt relief after being kept in suspense. 'Senkganang se nthola morulo – he who refuses me relieves me of a load.' They consoled one another with such phrases as: 'The gods have not liked.'

Mabongo had all his hopes of uniting with his parents dashed to pieces: 'My father will be more angered to know that my own daughter has refused to be married by Ndala's child. I got myself married to a woman he did not like. He said I must never come to his kraal. Now I must join the army. My boss wants me to be with him.'

He pined over his misfortune. He lost interest in his work and longed for the day when he would be in the army. Mr Tereplasky was a recruiting officer in the Native Military Corps and had promised to have him enlisted as soon as 'things are put right in the business'.

After Mabongo's departure, Martha and her mother lived by taking in washing and on a portion of Mabongo's salary that was sent to them.

Mathloare's health declined from month to month: 'I stand at the path before the sun comes out and go to sleep when the gods of this world are walking about. You have pierced my heart with a spear,' she told Martha. 'But for you, your father would not have thrown himself to the soldiers.' She would sigh and spit heavy saliva. 'This heart is going to kill me.'

'Ma,' Martha would look at her mother when she spoke thus: 'I shall go away from this house and give myself to any man. If I had married a man whom I did not like just because you and father wanted cattle I would have lived in sorrow. Ndala's child is not for me. My child will grow and work for me.'

'I love you my child. But I must tell you these things while I still breathe out air.'

She continued to get worse.

'Your mother must be removed to hospital,' said the doctor.

'No. No. I want my child to get a child before I die.' She would cover her face when the doctor persisted that she must go to hospital. 'They kill my people in hospital if they don't die quickly.'

Martha undertook to do all the washing herself, and when she was away old Mrs Mapena looked after her mother: 'I shall never desert you. Moipone is as my grandchild. The gods will be with you. You will see her child.'

The ambulance arrived one day. A white man in a white dust coat inquired for 'Ma-Maphonga.'

Tiny and the other children were playing outside. They stopped when they saw the ambulance and sorrowfully watched the two white men, dressed like doctors. When one asked for Ma-Maphonga Tiny wiped the tears from her face and began sobbing and crying from the bottom of her heart.

The Indian shopkeeper shut the doors of his shop as the van passed with the patient: 'Mama go to hospital. Very sick. Ali will pray for her.'

His father, wife and children took off their sandals and turned towards the sun, clasping their hands in supplication. They murmured inaudible words. Their lips moved fast. Their faces looked as pathetic as the moon, curved in mourning for a big chief.

Martha looked on as the white man, helped by Ma-Mapena, moved her mother from the bed to the van. Then she wept and wept until her heart felt like bursting: 'How shall I live without a mother or a father? My father has gone to fight.' She covered her face at the thought of soldiers killing one another. She had seen pictures of soldiers and read about their killings. She had also sung at the Mendi Memorial Day: 'Ke bana bana ba tsetseng metse a matala. Bashoele bothle. Bashoetse Afrika. Bashoetse tokoloho. – They have crossed the blue sea. They died all. Died for Africa. Died for freedom.'

'My father has gone to fight for white people yet they still ask the people for passes. Look how that missus pays for this washing!' She opened her purse and threw a ten shilling note on the floor: 'Washing and ironing – ten shillings!'

'Your mother will come back. The doctors say she has heart trouble. They will keep her in a house where there is not a lot of noise.' Ma-Mapena reassured Martha when she returned from accompanying Ma-Moipone to the hospital.

'We have come to this world but once. We nourish an ignorant hope that we may see things beautiful and bad to come. There is no knowing the day when our eyelids will close and our faces will gradually fade away from the memories of posterity.'

Ma-Mabongo died in the hospital a few days after being admitted. She died poor but she left a legacy for the white people – that her daughter remain a servant to them, a nanny, housekeeper, cook, even to the extent of opening and closing the gates for the master's car. She had cursed the 'missus' as le hulo – stingy, chobolo – cheeky, but all the same she ironed the master's shirts to the best of her ability.

'Siss, I iron her man's shirts nice. She sleeps and takes money for nothing. I am the wife and I get nothing.'

Mathloare had died and left her only daughter with two months to go before giving birth. Her last unspoken wish was: 'God, help my child to give birth. The child will take my place.' And she breathed her last breath and remained mute as a Pharoah's tomb.

Martha's former teacher organized a choir for the funeral. Most of the members were Martha's former school-mates. It was held on a Sunday so that more people could attend. The mourners were mostly the same people who met every Sunday in Doornfontein in a joyous mood, but on this particular Sunday they were sad and some of them had started weeping at their places of work. When seeing them in such grief, their mistresses had excused them earlier than usual from their duties. 'I am very sorry, my girl. Go and bury your sister.'

Even the birds in the gum trees around the graveyard seemed to be silent with grief. And the wild flowers which grew in abundance seemed to have been turned downwards by an unseen hand. The bees had flown away to look for honey in a place where there was no mourning.

The moruti carried out the ceremony in a befitting manner. After being introduced to the relatives of the deceased, the teacher took his place at the back of the choir, instead of conducting it.

> Down this grave lies the body cold and stiff.
> With pains and sorrow it was afflicted.
> Up there in the skies the angels' trumpets sing,
> Down here on Earth, the people mourn with tears.
> It should never happen again that the people suffer.

Chorus: God shall wipe away all tears. There shall be
no more death and pain, nor fear from hunger
and affliction.

The people wept and beat their breasts and called out the names of their dead. The priest tore the bible and cast it into the grave.

7

THE WAR RAGED, and the newspapers carried news of the lost and dead and captured. Mrs Tereplasky kept a constant watch on these columns. At first there had been regular correspondence from her husband: that he was keeping well and that Mabongo was always with him and had proved a comrade indeed. Then there was a lull for a long time. She began to fear an unknown disaster. The days went by and she heard nothing and saw nothing in the papers. When she went to inquire at the information office she was told, 'Everything is well.'

Martha received a letter addressed to her mother from her father, saying that they had been transferred to the North and that his former boss had turned out to be a true comrade. 'He sleeps with me in the same tent.'

One day the evening press carried a long list of casualties, lost and dead. Mrs Tereplasky read the columns voraciously. She rushed on to the letter 'T' among the dead and saw nothing of her husband's name. She read the casualties and saw nothing, and then she read 'Missing: Lazar Tereplasky No. N.M./1896.' She let the paper drop.

She had also bought an African weekly newspaper: 'If I find Mabongo's name it could indicate what has happened to Lazar.' She saw nothing in the 'M's among the dead and casualties, but when she moved on to 'Missing', sure enough, she found 'July Mabongo No. N.M./5678.' Then she felt relief that her husband could not be dead. 'They can't both be reported missing unless they have just not been seen. If they were dead in the enemy field the Red Cross would have reported to the South African Legation. Perhaps they have been captured and the list has not yet been sent off. The authorities do not take missing men seriously.'

After about two months she received a letter from the military authorities with the news that the Red Cross had traced her husband to a prisoner-of-war camp. Martha received a similar letter about her father, and wondered how many years it would be before she would see him again.

From the day of Martha's mother's death a group of women slept with her for many months. Ma-Mapena adopted Martha as her child. Ndala had performed the duties of a parent during the funeral and continued to pay occasional visits and to see that the rent was paid. He made weekly allowances to Martha.

Neighbours and other people gave handsomely and the shop-keeper, Mr Bhoola, gave a loaf of bread and other food-stuffs to the people who spent nights with Martha. 'Me make money, me must also give. Allah give more.'

Ndala used to entertain the women by telling them stories of ancient marriages. Martha had developed a parent-love for him. She found him to be more sociable than her father and felt that she had done the right thing by refusing the marriage proposal of his son.

'If I had accepted and the child did not look like Sephai they would have called me sebebe. My child would also have suffered by being called illegitimate: letla-leanya . . . came sucking!'

The women too would lie about the house and listen to Ndala:

'Once upon a time,' he would begin, 'a woman was married to a man whom she had never seen. The man's parents came to seek a wife and the girl agreed to be married to this man whom she had never seen. After giving ten head of cattle and some goats and sheep, they took her to her husband's place. A big feast was made and the girl was put in a small hut and told not to be afraid of anything that came to her. She sat in the hut and night came and everybody went to sleep in their huts. The poor girl slept but nobody came to her hut. The next morning, very early, she got up and went to fetch water from the river.

'Night after night she slept alone, and in the morning went to fetch water from the river. "Have you seen anything?" asked the old woman who was her mother-in-law. "I have seen nothing mother. Only water splashing from the centre to the banks and a wind blowing softly".

'She spent her days working in the house only, for she was not allowed to speak to other girls of her age. "When you have washed, tell me," her mother-in-law would order her to tell her when she had seen her periods. But she was still young and did not see womanhood. Month after month passed and another ploughing season came. The people went to plough and left her in the house. The poor girl stayed and became leaner and leaner, but she still went to the river every morning and saw the water splash and wet the banks.

'When the stalks of the mealies were tall and the grass in the evening was full of water, Masalanyana, for that was her name, saw her womanhood and told her mother-in-law, who said: "Don't go to the river tomorrow morning. I shall go and fetch water".'

'Ah!' sighed Martha, 'She was a cruel woman.'

'Yes, my child, people of the old times regarded their son's wives as makgoba – slaves. They had paid cattle for them. They had a big say about the way she had to work in the house and when to get children.'

'What happens if the husband dies?' asked Martha.

'Ah! my child, you should know that – the younger brother does not marry her but goes into the house in the evening and fathers the children for the dead brother, and the children call him Rangwane – young father. But I must go on with my story.

'One evening, when Masalanyana's mother-in-law had counted the days that must have passed since the girl's period, she instructed her not to close the door that evening and not to cry when she saw anything coming into her hut: "Your man will come. You must make blankets ready for him," were her instructions.

'The night came and the people in the village went into their huts and fastened the doors that night because the river did not ripple and they knew that something was going to happen.

'A big wind, and hot, blew in the village, and everybody covered their heads and blew out the lights and made sure that the doors were fastened inside. The village was as bright as day, even the baloi who are supposed to go about at night and terrorise sleepers did not go out.

'The wind passed from kraal to kraal and went towards Masalanyana's kraal of her marriage, and a big snake fell into her lapa.'

'Yoo! You frighten us,' cried the women.

'It rolled and rolled on the lapa because it was as slippery as the floor in white people's houses. Its eyes brightened the hut and the side lapas. It rolled and rolled and moved slowly towards the hut. Masalanyana saw it and saw that it could not move quickly, so she left the hut, jumped over the wall of the lapa and ran out of the village as fast as she could.

'She ran the whole night and the next morning when she was tired and the sun was too hot she rested in the big shade of the morula tree, and ate its fruit to satisfy her hunger and thirst. When the shadow grew short she ran on towards her home village.

'Her brother, who did not know her any more, ran to kill her for he took her to be moloi. "Kill the moloi," he cried to other boys. "Don't kill me," she sung. "I am Masalanyana, your sister. I was married to a snake. Don't kill me, Masalanyana."

'Her brother stopped and dropped his sticks. When they reached home everybody was pleased and a big feast was made for her. She was married to a chief and the chief sent some men to go and kill the snake. They brought back its eye, which looked like one of the stones with which white women decorate their fingers, and they made beautiful beads out of it for Masalanyana.'

'Ah!' cried the women. 'You have been brought up by grandmothers. They spend the nights telling nice stories and never tired of it.'

Martha thought that Ndala was making an example to her that if she had married without love for the man she would have led an unhappy life and ultimately been divorced.

In spite of her advanced state of pregnancy, Martha moved about energetically.

'Let me sing for you, father.'

'Ah! sing my child.'

Make me young to dance Marabi.
Prospect Township, Ma-Ndlovu's house was gorgeous.
At the side of George I danced and sang.
It was nice when Ma-Ndlovu's seepa mokoti served us with skomfana.
Oh! take me back to Marabi, take me back.

She swung from side to side as if there was nothing handicapping her. The people in the yard blocked the door and from the next yard others craned their faces over the corrugated fence, screaming at the top of their voices for repetition: 'Encore, encore, Moipone, hamba wena. Hamba ngoanyana wa Marabi – the Marabi girl.'

Martha sang again and a piano could be heard playing a few houses away. She fell into her old song: 'Tjeka-tjeka, ngoanyana wa Marabi Tjeka-tjeka sebebe, tjeka-tjeka meisie, tjeka-tjeka sebebe.'

'My son would have been lost if he had married such a woman. She is pregnant but still moves about like a springbok. What can a farm boy do with a town girl? She would leave him with the children in the night and go to Marabi. I shall tell my child not to be sorry about not marrying her. She is only good for town boys.'

'You talk to yourself, Ndala. Are you mad?' inquired a woman who had noticed him speaking aloud but to nobody.

It was usual for Ndala to consult his bones every morning for events of the day. On one particular morning he got up very tired and, according to his prediction, something was going to happen. He listlessly stretched his body and the joints cracked as if they were being dislocated. He felt pains: 'Pains like this are a sign that one of my relatives is sick.'

He fetched from a corner a jackal tail bag and from it he emptied bones. As they fell, one on top of another, he spoke to them: 'Bones of the dead, tell me what will arise today '

He shifted some from place to place: 'Makgolela – a prediction that the bones blame someone as the cause.'

He gathered them again into his hands and breathed into them: 'Tell me, the bones of the dead: lions, monkeys, kudu and others, who has fallen into the hands of the bathakati?'

He praised the wisdom of his forefathers for having given him knowledge to talk to the bones of the dead: 'Talk to the gods. Talk ye bones of the dead animals. Talk, you who are long dead. . . . Aaaa! They point out the balimo. This one still points at makgolela. There is a young woman in pains. Who is she?' He shifted the bones he had not touched. 'Someone who venerates Tlou, the elephant. This bone indicates a man from Bokone. A young man. He stabs at this woman. He is the one who causes her to have pains.' He inspected them sadly, meditating: 'It is Moipone who is in pains. The young man is the one who has spoilt her. He sleeps with other women and that makes Moipone get pains.'

He moved his fingers from bone to bone: 'Say, the bones of the dead. What is it that also keeps this young woman in pains? They tell again that it is balimo. It is a young woman who died with a pierced heart. She died wanting to see her grandchild. Her first grandchild.'

He searched among the herbs for an underpart of hippopotamus skin, and from a paper bag he took a handful of sand which he had preserved since the funeral of Martha's mother: 'The skin will lessen her pains and she will bathe with this sand from her mother's grave.'

Arkson & Son was one of the busiest shops in town. It specialized in selling to middle-class customers, and never bothered to attract prospective buyers from the street. Its salesmen merely came to work to spend time perusing the new catalogues from overseas and handing them over to the clerk to send to their customers. The people who came to the shop were mostly the wives of customers, coming to look at the latest styles.

Ndala sat outside the shop for the most part of the day, after cleaning the windows and dusting the shop. When lunch-hour came he went to his room at the back of the shop. On this particular day he hoped for a customer to give an order for delivery so that he could go and give Mrs Mapena the medicines needed to help Martha.

The hour passed and he returned from lunch. He sat outside the shop looking forward to closing time so he could get on to his bicycle and save his cousin's daughter.

'Ndala!' called out the salesman, 'Quick, take this parcel to Parktown. It's half-a-dozen suits. Leave them there. There is no need for you to come back.'

Ndala delivered the parcel and rushed to Doornfontein. Martha had been in pains since midnight. Many herbs had been tried but had failed to help her. She was tired and had not eaten the whole day. But she kept on walking about. The little money in the house had been used for rent and food. The neighbours talked about sending her to hospital but the old woman said that Martha wanted to have the baby at home because the hospital had killed her mother.

'When you are very sick in hospital and you worry them, they give you a poison so you will not worry them any more. It is the first time Moipone gets a baby and she will worry them. God will help us. The one there in the skies is not foolish.'

'You have been told by the balimo,' said the old woman when Ndala arrived. 'Your child has been in pains the whole night and the whole day.'

'I was told by my balimo. They told me that she was in pains and showed me what causes the pains. She will be alright before the sun goes down.'

'Moipone, my child,' said Ndala, as soon as he entered the house, 'I am your god. You are going to be alright now.'

He began unfolding little packages and ordered the old woman to prepare warm water. When the water was ready he boiled the hippopotamus skin in it. When it was cool he administered it to her. From the brown packet he poured the sand he had taken from her mother's grave into a small container and stirred it with water. He administered part of it to her and ordered the old woman to splash her body with the remainder.

'I am not a doctor. These things were given to me by balimo. They showed me that I must come and help this child.'

He left and said he would return in the morning.

Martha had more severe pains than before. They cut across her abdomen like a sharp edge of a razor. Then there was a lull as if everything was over, but the pain returned again like a flash of lightning.

'Ndala has given this child a poison,' said Ma-Mapena to herself. She went outside and gazed blankly at the sky. Then the cry of a baby could be heard. Without believing her ears she rushed back into the house. There, beside Martha, was a baby. It was crying as if cold water had been poured on to its naked body. It howled and howled and Tiny grew astonished as to whose baby could be in her uncle's house.

'Ah, I see.' She giggled into her blankets so that old Mapena should not hear her. 'Ausi Moipone has bought a baby.'

Martha slept the sleep of a drunkard and, when she awoke the following morning the child was sleeping by her side. She looked at it and wondered if she had really borne it. She remembered only the pains and the herbs.

'Is it my child?' she inquired from Ma-Mapena.

'No, it's not yours. It's Ndala's. He brought him into this earth.'

'What is it?'

'A boy. So Ndala has borne himself. His name is Ndala.'

Martha thought how old-fashioned the name was. Other boys would think he was a farm boy. 'Thula – keep quiet, Sonnyboy.' She gently brought the child to her breast and fed it. Her eyes were fixed on the baby. It sneezed. 'Balimo!' cried Ma-Mapena in thankfulness.

Sorrows that grieved my mind are now amended
Months ago I was orphaned and bereaved
And many nights I spent in meditation
And blankly cast to the skies.
Friends came to console me,
Many nights they spent with me,
Hunger they drove away, and thoughts that
Would have ruined me flew away.
Now at my side, tended and little,
A flesh of my own.
Day and night it cries, not bereaved but mothered,
Day by day it will grow and how sweet it will sound when
'Mama, mama' it calls,
All my sorrows, deep in the grave will descend
And never more be remembered,
This child will be my mother and father.

Africans look upon the birth of a child as a blessing. It is regarded as an asset to the family: 'I have borne myself a man. He will kill my enemies and he will work for me.' It is a general saying for Africans to express their gratitude for the new-born in this manner. When Martha awoke from her long and deep sleep she forgot all the curses she had uttered against George: 'I wish he would come and see the child. It looks like him.'

8

MRS TEREPLASKY, WHO was a trained social worker, had joined the organization that was concerned with the removal of Africans from the city slums to Orlando. She was the honorary secretary and took a deep interest in her work.

It was at the peak of the campaign to clear slums that Mrs Tereplasky came across the name of the Mabongos in a newspaper, reading that: 'Martha Mabongo is an orphan: her mother died six months ago and her father is a prisoner-of-war. She has a young baby. She was born in Johannesburg about eighteen years ago. She has no relatives . . .'

'Ah!' she sighed. 'This must be the daughter of July. I will ask one of the dairy boys to find out.'

The messenger she sent to find out about the Mabongos reported that Martha was July Mabongo's daughter and that her mother had died a few months ago. He also reported that the City Council would not give her a house without an assurance that the rent would be paid.

'Die kind is baie mooi, Missus – the child is very nice,' added the messenger.

'Did you tell her who I was?'

'No, Missus.'

'Very good. I don't want her to know who I am.'

As honorary secretary of the welfare society which was helping the slum-dwellers, Mrs Tereplasky revealed to the committee that Martha Mabongo's father had worked for her husband for many years and they were now together in the army: 'We must do all we can to get her a house in Orlando. I shall undertake to see that her rent is paid for several years.'

The committee agreed to have Martha's name included among those receiving food and clothing parcels and also to get in touch with employers who could give her a job after a few months, when her baby was old enough to be left at home.

Daily more yards were demolished. Old and smoky furniture was piled on the pavements waiting for removal to Orlando. Martha little thought that she too would one day move there: 'I can't get a house – no father, no mother.'

Then one day, after the welfare people had been to 26 Staib Street and put many questions to her, a young man on a bicycle brought a letter addressed to her. She had to sign for it. It said that she must report herself to the Orlando Office 'as soon as possible' with a letter addressed to the Superintendent.

The next day Martha left her six months old child with Ma-Mapena, as she expected to be away until evening. Martha lifted the child before going, and pressed him against her breast and kissed him. The African section of the Jeppestown Station where Martha bought her ticket, was built of corrugated iron. In the front was a brick wall with a small window for Europeans. After buying her ticket, she walked towards a group of women who were also waiting for the train to Pimville. The women were old and fat, young and lean, one of them distended with child but looking energetic. They all talked at the same time and laughed with their mouths wide open. At the approach of a stranger, they nudged each other's elbows and giggled. The oldest among them was chewing sugar cane, throwing the wastes on to the embankment.

'Lumela ngoana wa ka – good day my child,' greeted the eldest one.

'Age ma,' replied Martha with a smile.

'Whose child are you?' asked another woman next to the old woman.

'Mabongo,' replied Martha shyly.

The oldest woman, now having finished her sugar cane, joined in the conversation. She whispered to the nearest woman that the Mabongos were witch-doctors.

A woman who had been sitting next to Martha moved away from her, excusing herself by saying that she was going to the toilet. The pregnant woman bent forward from the waiting room seat and announced that the train was coming.

The booms lowered at the intersection of Commissioner Street. The cabin-bell sounded a warning of an approaching train. The women lifted their bundles of washing and got on to the train. The old woman who had been telling the others of the Ndebele witchcraft pushed her bundle of washing in first. She jammed the door shut, and seated herself nearest the door, panting loudly.

'Siss, white men have no respect for women,' she murmured to herself, in admonishment of the white train driver who had moved the train before all were seated. She took from her blouse a small tin of snuff wrapped in a dirty handkerchief and applied it to her nostrils with satisfaction, sneezed and thanked her grandfathers for having held the white guard against his evil intent. She blew her nose and splashed mucus from her bare hand on to the floor and wiped it with a big bare foot.

The pregnant woman had taken a seat opposite Martha. She busied herself with crochet work taken out from her bag, while Martha meditatively looked out of the window, gazing into the residential yards. Children, dressed in rags, dug for unknown treasures in the rubbish heaps. She had been at these rubbish heaps herself, searched for food in that same manner. 'I hope there are no heaps of rubbish in Orlando,' she said to herself. She had been told that there were beautiful houses there and that the streets were cleaned. The rent was about seventeen shillings and four-pence per month for a three-roomed house with a yard. She felt the letter kept in her bosom and sighed with relief that it was not lost. 'The white woman who sent that messenger is the one who is going to pay my rent,' she thought.

101

The train was nearing Doornfontein station and Mr Samson's double storey house was visible. Her thoughts were mixed, both sadness and longing rose in her. She pictured herself rehearsing in Mr Samson's study room, whispered her favourite song, 'Swing low, sweet chariot.' She took out from her bag a snapshot and held it in both hands. 'George, I loved you, but you have left me with a child.'

The pregnant woman, who had been sitting opposite her, recognized the young man in the snapshot as George, the Marabi player, a boy who had girls in almost every residential yard and was now working in Durban as a bus dispatcher. 'Poor girl, I wonder if she knows that George is in Durban. We women are fools, we fall in love with any man who is popular. They leave us with children and we have to bring them up alone.' She raised her eyebrows and studied Martha slyly. She remembered her as the girl who was to have sung at the Social Centre and had left with George before the programme had started. Her thoughts wandered to George as she had last seen him: dressed in cream flannel trousers with the bottoms upturned and twenty four inches wide; a white shirt with a silk hand-kerchief hanging loosely from his pocket, and a pair of white canvas shoes. She looked at Martha. 'It's Doornfontein Station.'

'Ja,' exclaimed Martha as if awakening from a sleep. She had been thinking about her son's likeness to George: thick lips, wide mouth, portly build and short. She had also wondered about the prospect of getting the house in her name. 'The Municipality wants one who has a man. He must have a pass. Must be working in Johannesburg for many years. George would be alright. He is Johannesburg born.' Tears, unnoticed by the other women, had stained her eyes. George felt like a spear in her heart. She debated within herself the possibility of being accepted as a child of Mapena, if the Old Mapena agreed to have the house registered in his name. 'He won't refuse because the rent is going to be paid by some kind white people. He will save enough money to go back to the farm.'

'I seem to know your face,' said the pregnant woman, after clearing her throat by coughing.

'My name is Martha. What is yours?'

'Mine is Sophie. Where did you attend school?'

'Albert Street School,' replied Martha with a clear voice.

'Do you know George?' asked Sophie.

Martha looked down at the floor. As the train started to move it seemed as though the swerving of the carriages from side to side were mocking at her. The cabin bell sounded, tolling the ignominious message of George deserting her. A hope flashed within her, as the booms began to leave the ground on the passing of the last carriage, that George would return to her one day. 'Those booms rise like someone who has gone to sleep and rises in the morning to work. George will surely come back.'

Sophie wondered whether the girl had heard her question.

'Do you know George?' she asked again, very slowly this time.

'Yes, I know him. He was my jong. I have a child by him.'

'That's nice.'

'Sophie!' exclaimed Martha seriously. 'You speak like someone who has never been left by a man. It's nice to have a child with someone who cares for it. But a man who has made you pregnant and then runs away, is no man. George ran away the same day I told him I was pregnant. He never even told his friends he was leaving. He left the good work he was doing. He was a clerk where he was working. Nice work to work with a tie on. But he left it because I told him I was pregnant. I don't know where he is. Is that nice?'

'I am sorry for you Martha. I know George from school. He was in love with many girls. He had girl friends at all the schools: Spes Bona, St. Cyprians, Albert Street, and all other schools. He was a champion at Marabi. All the girls cried for him. Yo-Yo,' she exclaimed, biting her thumb against her fourth finger, 'The kitchen girls. The kitchen girls all worked for him. They bought him suits and he collected money from them every month.'

'I don't care for town boys any more,' said Martha. 'I want any kind of man, I want a man who can work for me. I have had enough of Marabi. I have had enough of singing. I am now the mother of Sonnyboy. George will always remain a father of nobody.'

'I am very sorry to have told you all these things about George. I shouldn't have. He is the father of your child. You and he have given blood. You will always feel for him. My man likes girls too. When someone speaks bad of him I get angry. He is very educated. He passed matric at the college. He is a big mabalane, a clerk at the Municipal offices. All the municipal police call him "Nkosi". They give him money when they want to be made sergeants and he tells the Superintendent that the man is very good, and the Superintendent says: "All right Philip".'

Martha thought to herself that here was an opportunity to ask this woman to introduce her to her husband, so that she could be attended to without waiting like the other people who would be at the office.

'Sophie,' asked Martha shyly, 'can you introduce me to your man? I am going to ask for a house. I have a letter from some white people. Your man might help by attending to me first.'

Sophie kept quiet for a few moments. She felt a burning in her heart: such a nice girl would attract her husband. 'I don't like him to see pretty girls. One look at them is enough for him to propose. He speaks nice English. And his nice figure, tall. . . . My Philip even swanks when he walks. No wonder girls like him.'

Martha read her thoughts. 'She thinks I'm a cheap line to accept all ragtimes. I only want her to help me. I have had enough of ragtimes. George was enough. Teachers have proposed to me. I could have taken Mr Samson, a better man than all these. I didn't want to take someone else's man. His wife would have cried and cried and made bad luck for me.'

'I only want your man to help me to be attended to first. I must be back home before sunset or my child will cry for me. Grandmother does not like me to go about at night. She says we young women go out and get bad milk for the children, then their legs look like sticks. I want my child to grow fat, my dear.' She said this to show Sophie that she had discovered her jealousy.

'We shall find him still having his lunch,' said Sophie. 'Then I can introduce him to you and I shall wait outside the office. When the office opens and the policeman has taken you to your house, I shall leave you.'

The old woman with the bundle of washing raised her face and with an angry glare cast a warning eye upon the two young women speaking. 'Girls of today speak about men in the presence of adults. Siss, they can never keep husbands.'

The train steamed into Park Station and stopped to take more passengers. Women with bundles of washing balanced on their heads, small boys with boxes of sweets for sale and men with worn out faces and tattered trousers jostled into the coaches and took seats or remained standing.

'All tickets. Alle kaartjies,' shouted the ticket examiner.

The fat woman thrust her hand into her shirt blouse then into her skirt pockets, pulled off her headgear and dived down once more into her shirt blouse feeling her breasts and the tops of her arms. 'Molimo!' she cried, 'what has gone into my body?' She glared at the young women who had been speaking since the train had left the Jeppestown Station.

'They have talked so much that I have forgotten where I put my ticket! Rubbish children who talk about men. Au! Tsamaya baas – go away.'

'I am not going to move before I get a ticket from you. Toe maar, staan op.'

She began searching from pocket to pocket, pulled off her headgear and searched into her woolly, uncombed hair. Triumphantly she produced the ticket. 'Haa! You wished that I would not find it!'

The train had by now passed many stations and was nearing New Canada Junction. Martha pushed her head through the window. A group of miners returning home stood on the platform with heavy baggage: box trunks, suitcases, blankets folded into canvas covers, bicycles ornamented with hooters, mirrors, bells, blue and red stop lights; ail of them talking at once in a language alien to those on the train. Their trousers were patched with many colours of cloth and fastened with straps below the knees. To complete the attire, a pair of spectacles dangled over their noses so that they pitched their eyes over the frames to look at the passengers whom they hailed as 'daley kamina.'

Martha thought of Tiny's father who had returned from the mines to die. 'Are these men also returning to their homes to die?' The train puffed out of the station and left the miners struggling to board a stationary train which had just pulled on to the platform.

Philip was in the habit of taking lunch in his office where he continued his studies. His wife did not expect to find him outdoors. She was relieved at this thought, for she planned to see Philip before she introduced Martha to him.

'We are nearing Orlando Station. Philip will be in his office.' Sophie smiled and twisted her lips as though she wanted Philip to kiss her. 'I am the only one allowed to see him in the office during the lunch hour.' Martha nodded.

Martha and Sophie alighted and headed for the office where Philip worked. Women with colourful blankets walked from the station while others remained and squatted on the platforms laughing as hard as possible at the mine workers who seemed to be making eyes at them. The brightly patterned blankets of the men swept the ground as they walked leaving a trail of dust behind them. Some of the women swung their dresses towards the men and showed attractive legs and thighs. 'Manyeu, my father wants cattle,' they cried.

The driver, having alighted from the engine, joined the vanman in the nearest hut and demanded a measure of kaffir-beer and promised to pay at the end of the month.

'Die Mosotho meid is mooi!' the vanman exclaimed as the woman stooped to scoop from the can another measure of beer. The engine driver reminded him that the law forbade miscegenation. 'Ag! that's nothing, nature does not care for law.' The two drank and drank jug after jug of beer till they became drunk and interfered with the woman. 'Tsamaya – go. You want my husband to kill me!' she screamed and pushed the men out of the hut.

Martha and Sophie moved to the farther side of the station. Someone was playing a concertina, pulling and pushing the musical box with abandon. The white guard clutched at a Mosotho woman, laid his head on her breast like a baby and moved as though his boots pinched his feet while he danced.

'White men!' cursed an old woman. 'They like our women but they don't like our men to like theirs. Siss!'

Martha and Sophie walked towards the Municipal building. As they drew near they noticed a woman and a man sitting in the shade of a gum tree. The man's head was on the woman's lap. His long legs were stretched out before him and his face was turned like a lamb's towards the woman who bent down gently and kissed him and smoothly ran her hand over the man's head. The man seemed to be in a daze as he passed his hands down her breasts, the fingers seeming to be fishing for something.

'Oh! darling, I love you very much. I have never loved a woman as I love you.'

'You are a liar, Philip, you love your wife more than you love me.'

'No, my dear.' He curled his fingers round her bosom. 'I don't love her. I was forced to marry her. If I refused her after she had fallen pregnant I would have lost my job. The priest that got me this job said that I was to behave.'

'Did you pay lobola?' asked the mistress.

'I paid after I had married her at the Native Commissioner's office and at the Church. I paid eighty pounds in instalments. Now I am penniless. I have to feed the kid and now she is going to have another baby. Who knows that it is I who gave her the baby this time?'

'So Philip, if you make me pregnant, you will deny it. You will say the teachers have done it because I work at the school.'

'Ag! man, don't talk nonsense. You I love.' He closed his eyes and placed his hands on her buttocks and pretended to be asleep.

'Mehlolo!' exclaimed a woman walking ahead of Martha and Sophie. 'Marabi love – men and women kissing each other in front of everybody.'

'Aunties of today are inquisitive,' said Sophie softly for fear the woman might hear her. 'It's not her business if people love each other. She should mind her own business.'

'They are deeply in love,' answered Martha.

'Jo-jo-jo! My husband!' Sophie fell on the couple like a sack of potatoes and ripped the woman's blouse from top to bottom. Her nails penetrated the woman's face and the blood flowed freely.

'Fighting! Fighting!' screamed the school children from all over.

'Hit her, Mistress,' yelled the little ones dancing around as the two women fell upon each other. The teacher unlocked herself from Sophie's grip, backed a little and plunged with full force into her opponent. Sophie whirled to the ground like a knocked-out boxer. The little ones danced. 'That's right, Mistress. Knock her with your shoe.' She pulled off her shoe which descended upon Sophie's head, the blood gushing out like a stream of water. 'Now kick her, Mistress.' Before the teacher could lift her leg Martha threw her heavy body against her and they landed far from the scene of the fight. Martha brought her to the ground and pressed her throat until she almost choked. 'Ausi, Ausi, please leave me!' begged the teacher and Martha loosened her grip.

During the fight Philip locked himself in his office and watched the women from the window. 'Let them fight. I don't care.' The Superintendent called him. 'I am told those women were fighting over you, Philip?'

'I don't know Sir. I only saw them fighting.'

The police guard boastfully entered the office, saluted the Superintendent and looked at Philip with scorn.

'Sir, some women have been fighting for Philip. His wife has been taken to hospital. The doctor says the baby may die before it is born.'

'And what did you do when you saw them fighting?' asked the Superintendent with a sly smile.

'I did nothing Sir. I like to see the women showing their bloomers.'

'And what else did you want to see?'

'Nothing, Sir.' The policeman showed some embarrassment.

Turning to the policeman the Superintendent barked: 'Do you get paid to watch people fight in the streets and do nothing about it? Get out of my office! Philip, get me through to Head Office. I won't keep fools as policemen in this township. Get me another police boy from Number Two office.'

The policeman who was ordered out of the office was told to report the next morning without his uniform and Philip was told to resume his duties: 'Our work won't be stopped by women who like to fight for men', scowled the Superintendent.

After the fight, Martha took her seat among the women who waited. Philip recognized her as the one who had helped his wife during the fight and was afraid that she might cause him trouble. He hesitated a few moments before deciding whether to let her wait until her turn came or to call her immediately. He moved his pens and pencils from side to side and peeped through the window every so often to see if she had left. 'I think I'd better call her in,' he said to himself.

'Poyisa, call that girl in.'

Martha faced Philip unperturbed.

'What do you want?'

She felt her blouse and took from it the letter sent to her by some white person to hand to the Superintendent at Orlando Township.

'Where did you get that letter from?' Philip's fingers trembled as he extended his hands to receive it.

'It was given to me by some white people so that I might get a house here.' Martha was worried that her participation in the fight might jeopardize her chances of obtaining a house. Philip took the letter and handed it to his superior. The Superintendent read the typewritten letter and indicated to Philip that he was satisfied.

'How old are you?'

'Eighteen years, baas,' replied Martha.

'Are you married or have you a man?'

'No Sir. I stay with people I call grandfather and grandmother. My mother is dead and my father has joined the soldiers.'

'How can I let a child like you live in a house alone? You must get some man to register the house in his name.'

'You may put the house in my grandfather's name.'

The Superintendent beckoned to the clerk. 'Poyisa, take this girl and the other people to the houses. Let Philip give you the list.'

107

'Right, Nkosi.' He saluted and disappeared into the interior of the township with a group of women.

The Black Jack clerk was followed by scores of women, and Martha darted from one block of houses to another.

'Ma-Dhlamini, here is your house.' He walked as fast as his legs would stretch, leaving the women far behind to catch up with him at another range of houses.

'Ma-Thusi, here is your house.'

Martha began to be worried. 'Perhaps the old man's name was not acceptable. They said I must have someone registered for the house.' There were still some women following the Black Jack. 'I should not worry. These women are not disturbed.' She trudged along waving the long-grass aside as she walked.

'Look out for the snakes,' shouted the Black Jack.

'You have brought us here to be eaten by snakes,' a chorus of voices responded.

'Allida Mokwena. Here is your house.'

'Dankie Morena, I had no more hope that my name would be called.'

'I think the next one is mine,' thought Martha.

'Martha Ma..a..a..a..bongo. I cannot pronounce your surname properly. Here is a paper which says if you don't bring a man's name before the end of the month your name will be removed from the list.'

Martha sighed a breath of relief. She entered the house, a three-roomed house, the lavatory a few feet away. She had never known a house with more than one room, and with a lavatory for each family. 'A house. . . . I am dreaming. This room will be mine and my child's. Perhaps Tiny will sleep with me. The old man and grandmother will sleep in that one.' She walked into the room and felt over the walls with her palms. 'They are rough.' She rubbed her feet on the floor. 'Dusty.' She spread her arms across the doorway. 'No doors. Too narrow for furniture to go in.' She looked up at the rafters and saw a spider. 'In the missus' house where I do washing there is a white ceiling and there are no spiders. If a man quarrels with his wife he will hang himself. Those beams make me frightened.' She walked out.

'Yooo! What is that?' The policeman said they were to look out for snakes. A chameleon steadily moved through the grass. Martha had never seen such a creature in her life. 'It walks like someone who wants to steal. I think it gets into the houses when people are in bed. I won't let Tiny play with Sonnyboy outside.'

She sat on the doorstep watching the chameleon, and murmuring:

I have from childhood to womanhood lived in the slums,
On heaps of refuse for food and play did I contend.

Carcass of dogs and cats with refuse intermingled;
Oh! God, what a smell, but for food I did persist.
Gods whose faces are black, turn not away from me,
Palm with thy hands the body that for years has suffered.

She awoke from the reverie as if she had been violently shaken. 'I have been dreaming. It is the fight that has made me sleepy.' She boarded a late train back to Jeppestown and on arriving home saw Tiny waiting for her at the gate.

'Sonnyboy has been crying the whole day. Grandpa and Grandmother have gone to look for you at the Marabi Dance.'

'Voetsek, Tiny, I am not a Marabi girl.'

When she entered the house, her grandparents had already returned from all the yards where they knew the Marabi Dance to be popular. 'Her mother has left trouble for us,' sighed the grandmother. 'Molimo! Where have you been, Moipone? You go about at night and don't behave like a woman who has a child.' Martha told her about her journey and what was required for the house to be registered.

'Moipone, I have spoken to your grandfather. He has agreed to write his name for your house. But we shall only stay a short time with you because the old man wants to go and die at home.'

Tiny laughed when she heard that they were going to stay in Orlando with Martha. 'Ausi Martha,' she said, 'I am going to belaga Sonnyboy. I won't go to school any more. When he is big I will go to school with him.' She knelt down to the child. 'Thula Sonnyboy. Mama is going to buy you sweets.'

She began to sing: 'Jack and Jill went up the hill to fetch a pail of water. Jack fell down and Jill came tumbling after and Jack broke his leg.'

'Tiny! Who taught you that song?' inquired Martha, surprised to hear Tiny sing in such perfect English.

'Mistress Nancy,' replied Tiny. 'I can sing another one: Kusasa, kusasa, vukani bantwana – tomorrow, tomorrow, get up children, kudu-kudu, vukani bantwana.'

'Tiny, when I work I am going to buy you a dress. You must look after Sonnyboy.'

'Ausi Moipone, I am no more going to play Black Maipatile. When we are in Orlando I shall go to the bioscope with him.'

'There is no bioscope in Orlando,' intervened Martha.

'I shall go to Marabi then.' She giggled and looked stealthily at Martha. 'I will kick you Tiny.'

'Hau! I didn't say you go to Marabi. I said aubuti George.' She looked from side to side as if searching for the person talked about. 'He is going to play the piano for Ma-Ndlovu.'

'Tiny, jy is stout, you are naughty.'

'Alright, Ausi Moipone. I shall go to the farms with Sonnyboy . . . that whiteman who came to marry you.'

Martha smacked her and pushed her outside: 'If you don't stop talking rubbish I won't buy you a nice dress.'

'Alright Ausi Moipone, I have finished talking.'

It was on a Monday morning, while most people were still asleep, that the first convoy of Municipal trucks turned into Sivewright Avenue and some drove along Angle Road and then into Staib Street and stopped in front of two yards: the Makapan and Molefe yards. A team of workmen began knocking on the doors of those who were still abed.

'Vula mama. Waar is jou papier?'

The African labourers and the white drivers took turns to wake and demand removal documents.

'Hau, baas, my kind het nog nie geëet nie–my child hasn't eaten yet,'

'Hiakona lo sebensa kamina – not my business.'

The labourers began piling household belongings on the pavement. The little ones held on to the skirts of their mothers and one white driver frightened them by showing his false teeth: 'Don't frighten my child, masepa a gogo.'

'Jou papier meid,' demanded a driver arrogantly of Martha.

'Kan jy nie mooi praat nie?' she protested. 'Can't you speak nicely?'

'Kaman, I don't care about nice.'

He scanned the papers and looked Martha over from head to foot: 'You are a lucky girl to have a white person to pay your rent. These kaffirboeties spoil the kaffirs. I wish I could make the laws. I would send every kaffir to work on the white farms. They are going to live in houses like those of the white people.'

'Jim,' he called to one of his African men, 'see that this meid gets her rubbish outside quick.'

Piles and piles of furniture, pots, clothing and other home utensils were scattered about the pavement whilst the officials checked the papers and the row of rooms being vacated. The demolishing squad began wrecking the iron-sheet houses as if they had been children's playing houses, merely perched on the ground. Here and there a rodent ran out for its life, cockroaches climbed the trousers of the workmen and one of them was seen running away: 'Mamolapo, mamolapo,' and he refused to return to the demolishing: 'Haikona baas, ena hambili pakate lo trousers kamina – no baas, it has got into my trousers.' His eyes protruded and his body shivered as if the cockroach was still moving in his trousers.

Martha, with the baby on her back, the old woman and Tiny climbed on to the back of the lorry. Martha looked at the place where she had lived since a child, perhaps two or three years older than her baby. She did not remember how she came to the place. She had been told that she was born in Sophiatown and that her mother later went to live in Klipspruit (Pimville) when the big sickness nearly killed them. She did not remember Pimville. 'I don't like Sophiatown,' and she blushed when she thought of the night spent there with George.

Then her mind turned to her dead mother. She could picture her entering the yard: 'Moipone, my child, you have not yet cooked. Your father is going to kill us. Make quick, my child.' The unsaid words rang in her ears. She pushed her finger into one ear and shook it violently. 'Perhaps,' she thought, 'my mother's ghost will come tonight and find us gone.' She wept.

'What is it, Moipone?' asked the old woman, Ma-Mapena.

'Nothing.'

'Why then do you cry?'

Martha wiped her eyes.

'I think she is thinking about her mother,' said the old woman to herself. 'She grew up in this place and became a woman here. It is sad to leave your old home.'

The lorry left town and snarled around the mine dumps. It stopped at a gate and the driver handed a bundle of papers to an African policeman who then ran as fast as he could to the office, returning some time later.

'Turn down that road, baas, then turn again down that road, baas, then turn again down that one. You will see the house.'

'Alright, Jim.' The driver drove off.

'White people have no respect. He calls me Jim. One day I shall fix them up. I shall be the baas. Then I shall say, "run boy, kaman run!" and if he doesn't run I shall kick him on his buttocks.' The policeman lifted his knobkerrie and brandished it in the direction of the disappearing truck: 'Pas-op! – Look out!'

When the men had begun to stream out of the yards for work that morning there was much murmuring: 'We shall never see this place again.'

'How are we going to find our new houses?'

They walked as if their feet were heavy and lowered their heads as if in mourning: 'The white people are chasing us far from town. How are we going to pay for the train? Here in town we don't pay anything for going to work, we just walk and at lunch time we get back and eat at home.'

The women, however, took the matter humorously. They danced about and consoled each other with the thought that in the new place their children would not find it easy to go to Marabi.

'The Municipality does not allow houses to be turned into Marabi halls.'

They teased their husbands, saying that if they did not come home that night they would take a white driver for the night: 'Wa mona – have you seen him?' A fat young woman put her arm around the neck of the driver and he, ashamed, pushed it away. The young husband answered back that if this happened he would kill him.

There were some women who seriously feared that their husbands would find an excuse for not coming home. Their men would sleep in the suburbs because they had no money for train fare, or could not find the house.

'Oh ya! Today you will find a good chance of going to your kitchen woman. You will see me if you don't come home,' one woman pointed a warning finger at her man.

The day passed, ending in a bustle and hurry. Bewildered workers rushed for trains to Orlando and, in confusion, some took Randfontein trains and were ordered to pay extra or get off: 'Kan jy nie lees nie?' – can't you read?' Some passed the station and went on to Pimville where the residents laughed at them as 'baris, greenhorns from Doornfontein.'

There were some however who did not believe that the removal would take place: 'They can't load everything in one day and where will they find houses to give everybody?' They came back to their old abodes and found heaps of corrugated iron sheets, and, because it was already late, they gathered enough irons to make a shelter for the night and started to cook meals in tins. The policemen on duty noticed the smoke and, finding people, arrested them and charged them with trespassing: 'You have no right to be here. Your place is in the Native Location. The Government and the Municipality have built nice houses for you but you still want to make the whiteman's place stink.'

The domestic workers heard from their mistresses that 'Natives' had been removed many miles from town but they could not understand how hundreds of people could be removed in one day or two to a place so far away. When Sunday came-they gathered in the streets as usual and those who drank quenched their thirst from some women who had come back on Sunday to carry on with their business.

Martha felt for the first time the pleasure of living in a house with rooms. She had grown up in what was called a house, but here was a real house. Three rooms: a kitchen and two bedrooms, one which she shared with Tiny and her child and the other where the old Mapenas slept. The kitchen served as a sitting room for strangers and when she had important visitors she let them sit in her room. Sonnyboy and Tiny found a lot of space to play in in the house. There was a big yard where vegetables and flowers could be grown. In the first week after their arrival the old man prepared the ground for planting.

Martha had last been in the house the day she had travelled to Orlando with Sophie and the other washerwomen. She had inspected each room but felt differently now as she slept in and cleaned the house. She felt that it was hers. 'It is in my grandfather Mapena's name but it is mine. The man who came to me saying he was sent by the white woman my father worked for, told me that the missus was going to pay the rent. So the house is mine.'

* * * * *

112

The years passed by and the three years of free rent ended. Old Mapena and his family had gone back home. When they left Martha, with a relative to look after her, they wished her all the badimo – blessing: 'Look for a good man to marry you. You have seen how Marabi boys do – they run away and leave you alone with a child.'

After feeling a short period of loneliness, Martha had got used to being left alone. She had a sleep-out job and on weekends did a few bundles for her late mother's European customers.

One day, when returning from work, the memories of the old days clouded her thoughts. She saw herself at Ma-Ndlovu's Marabi Dance, with George playing 'Sonnyboy'.

'If he could know that I have borne a son for him called Sonnyboy he would play it madly.'

Then the words began to come back to her: 'Climb up on my knee, Sonnyboy. You are only three, Sonnyboy. There's no way of saying, there's no way of mourning. What. . . .'

'Pii.' A black big car stopped alongside her and its driver apologized for startling her.

'Are you not Martha?'

'Yes, that's me.'

'I am George's friend who took you to Sophiatown.'

'I am sorry, I didn't recognize you. It's been a long time. My boy is ready for school.' She laughed and spat on the ground. 'You men are dogs. You bear children all over and leave them like rats. You helped George to take me to Sophiatown and when you saw that I was pregnant you tipped him off to run away. Now that you see my child is big you want to tell him to come back.'

'Martha, George did not tell me that he was leaving Johannesburg. I only heard that he was in Durban. He didn't tell anybody, he just got out.'

'One day, one day, he will think about me and he will say: "Martha, please help me," and his own child will tell him to go to hell.' She beat her skirt with her palms: 'Backside!' and she walked away.

When the Orlando train arrived, Martha and the other passengers scrambled into it, pushing each other aside to get a seat. They all talked at the same time as if in emulation of one another, or like hecklers trying to silence a speaker. In the tumult hawkers were selling wares – sweets, herbs, handkerchiefs, peanuts and all the other assortment of goods one finds in the Indian market. The ticket examiners beat the wooden seats and demanded tickets. Where they were not produced and money was paid instead, the ticket examiner pocketed it and passed by without writing out a ticket.

In 1945 the war ended and not long afterwards Mabongo returned to South Africa with a group of other ex-prisoners-of-war. They were welcomed at Johannesburg station and, led by a Native military band, marched along Von Weillich Street and into the Bantu Sports Ground where they were thanked and dismissed.

Through the Red Cross, the relatives of the returning men had been notified. Martha met her father after the dismissal. But July had aged a great deal, and daughter and father met as strangers. They remained so, because, after Mr Tereplasky's return, Rooiveldt Daries opened new branches in various parts of the country and July was sent as 'boss-boy' to the East London branch.

Martha was used to travelling on the Orlando train. The long journey was no longer tiresome. It was nothing strange to see mine recruits carrying loaves of bread under their armpits, nor to see them waiting at New Canada station half-clad in calico cloth. It was still somewhat spectacular to see the Portuguese Africans dressed in fancy silks and dancing on the platforms as if they were happy to leave for their homes, or to be safe from a mine rockfall.

'Tiny's father left many years ago because he complained that the mines make a man work too hard for very little money. I think these men are also glad that they are going back home.'

In less than five minutes the train stopped again, at Mlamkuzi station, then it arrived at Orlando. There was a scramble and pushing to get out. 'Joo, my washing is in the train!' A washerwoman cried for the white people's washing she had left in the train. She had not forgotten it. She had pushed it as far as the door, alighted and turned to take the bundle out, but before she could reach it the train had pulled off. Martha and the others, having alighted, each took his or her own direction into the township.

It was late in the afternoon when Martha reached her gate. She opened the letter-box and found a letter bearing a Durban postmark. When she got into the house and found a seat she carefully tore off the end of the envelope and pulled out the contents. Her heart beat fast and she perspired.

'Morena! It is George! Oh Morena wa ka – my lord. Where does he come from? Seven years. Sonnyboy already goes to school.' She pressed the letter against her heart and wept.

'Dearest Martha, I have been in Durban for a very long time. I have seen many women but they have never satisfied my heart.'

Then he went on to tell her how he still loved her and would like to come back to Johannesburg.

'My heart does not give me rest when I think that I have a child with you. Martha, please tell me if it is a boy, I had a dream that it was a boy.'

He related how the Bus Company had wanted to use him as an informer on other workers. That he would rather walk the streets without work than sell his own people.

'Our men have formed a trade union and have made some demands to the Company for more money and shorter working hours. The Company

114

is dead scared to meet the workers' representatives, so they want to use some of us to say who are the leaders.

'Martha, I want to come back to Johannesburg. I can always make a living without begging for work. I have done wrong to you, but I was still young and had not seen enough of life.'

It was a two-page letter. She read it over and over again, then her tears fell like a torrent of rain and blotted the words, and the pages fell from her hands.

'What is it Mama?' Sonnyboy looked up at his mother.

'Your father will come.' She brushed his woolly head, and began to speak to herself: 'God was not a fool to make black people. We are made out of the same river mud as the white people. The world was made for us all to live in and like each other.' She stopped and looked at her son.

'My child, you are going to grow to be a man. George, your father, wants to leave work because he does not want to sell his people. I like him for that. Our people must talk without being heard by the white people. Some tell the white people what we have said and are given money. Last night the people talked about schools and high rent, and this morning some people were arrested. You, you my child, must be a man.'

She rested her head on the table and wept.

Epilogue

MR TSHIRONGO SPENT a few months with his wife and children and then left them to look for work in Salisbury. He found employment with a white minister as a cook. His duties included cleaning the church and outbuildings. During church services Tshirongo would pretend to busy himself in one of the buildings so that he could see how the minister conducted the service. He gained more knowledge of the bible and of hymns.

'I am the way and the life.'

He spent his days off conducting services for the domestics on the outskirts of the town and became popular as umfudzisi. Some of the workers recognized him as the Right Reverend Ndlovu of Prospect Township in Johannesburg.

His master marvelled at the bible knowledge of the man, so he encouraged him to attend a night school conducted for African domestic workers.

'I am now a better Mfundisi than Bishop Mtembu. I can read and write.'

He had preached about St. Matthew, chapter five, but had never thought deeply about the meaning of the words until he learned to read them himself:

'And seeing the multitudes He opened his mouth. . . .

"Blessed are the meek for they shall see the kingdom of God."

'My people are suffering. They own nothing on this earth. This bible is wrong to tell us we must be meek so that we shall enter the Kingdom of God.'

His living quarters became a popular centre for religious and political discussions. Some maintained that Moses was a political leader of the children of Israel and that Tshirongo was a big Mfundisi who would call upon the Gods of the Africans to guide the people to freedom.

'My people, here in the British Empire, do not work in the towns for long periods. One teaches them this and that, tomorrow they go home. In Johannesburg people stay for a long time in town. They know how to fight for the kingdom in this world. I must go back to Johannesburg.'

He signed a service contract with the Wenela, the mine labour recruiting board—on the Rand. After two months on the mines he made inquiries about Ma-Ndlovu. He learned that she had left for Durban soon after he had absconded with her money. George's mother had moved to Prospect Township to avoid forced removal to Orlando, where there was no business. The other women talked of Ma-Ndlovu as a nodindwa. The poor Shangaan, Alberto, had left for his home to avoid bad luck from a woman whose husband had died. Other people avoided coming near her door because they said there was a spook in her room. Furthermore, the Police Station commander of Prospect Township had been transferred to Orlando and had made no further inquiries about Reverend Ndlovu. It was in fact said that he had remarked that the Reverend 'het haar reg gemaak. He has fixed her. She is a whore.'

So Ma-Ndlovu had left Johannesburg and gone to make a new life in a place where her evil ways were unknown.

The Reverend felt satisfied that he was no longer a wanted man. On his off shift days he went to Orlando and organized his congregation and on Sundays he conducted services. The congregation remarked on the way the Reverend did this: first the Lord's Prayer, then a hymn according to the church calendar year and then a sermon related to their living conditions. There was no more beating of drums and wild praying. He preached to his congregation that the white people had no moral right to prevent the Africans from living where they chose. He called his new church the 'Church of Africa'.

'The white Mfundisi I worked for had a church for the English people, why shouldn't I also have a church for Africans? The white Christians say, "Love thy neighbour as thyself" and yet they don't love us.'

Reverend Ndlovu still had his certificate, given to him by the Right Reverend Mtembu of Bethal and signed by the Native Commissioner of the same district: 'I hereby certify that the Right Reverend A. B. Ndlovu is ordained as a minister of the church. He has the right to baptise and perform marriages.'

Furnished with this certificate Reverend Ndlovu performed marriages and baptised in the name of the Father, the Son and the Holy Ghost.

'God created a man and a woman to bear the fruits.'

The church bell rang at eleven o'clock and the school children were given time off. The women wagged their tongues about. Young women who were not yet married scoffed: 'She will be divorced tomorrow.' Bus drivers formed an arch. The musicians played their best tunes. The school choir sang their best songs. There was however a lone marabi dancer who was asked to leave the church.

Reverend Ndlovu led the couple into the church chamber. Behind them Tiny lightly held the wedding dress and a boy of not more than seven years walked softly behind the man.

The woman whose dress Tiny held wept for joy that her dream of a lifetime had become reality. 'Oh George, you have come back.'

'George Sibeko, do you love this woman?'

'Yebo, Mfundisi.'

'Martha Mabongo, do you love this man?'

'E'ng, Moruti.'

'God has so desired that these two people should love each other that through God's love they become husband and wife.'

The Reverend closed the bible.

'God visited Abraham in a dream. "Abraham, go to the land of your fathers and take a wife".'

THE AFRICAN WRITERS SERIES

The book you have been reading is part of Heinemann's long-established series of African fiction. Details of some of the other titles available in this series are listed below, but for a catalogue giving information on all the titles available in this series and in the Caribbean Writers Series write to: Heinemann International Literature and Textbooks, Halley Court, Jordan Hill, Oxford OX2 8EJ;
Heinemann Educational Books Inc, 361 Hanover Street, Portsmouth, NH 3801–3959, USA.

BIYI BANDELE-THOMAS
The Man Who Came in from the Back of Beyond

Maude, a strange schoolteacher, tells the tale of a man from his girlfriend's past. As the naive student Lakemf listens, a tale of incest and revenge slowly begins to unfold.

CHENJERAI HOVE
Shadows

As the war for liberation rages around them, two young Zimbabweans must decide whether they will continue to live and love in such a barren land. A telling portrait of rural life and the strictures of colonial law.

NIYI OSUNDARE
Selected Poems

This collection contains the very best of Osundare's poetry. The verse testifies to his commitment to a popular 'total poetry' – words to be listened to in conjunction with song, dance and drumming.

TIYAMBE ZELEZA
Smouldering Charcoal

Two couples live under the rule of a repressive regime, and yet their lives seem poles apart. In this compelling study of growing political awareness, we witness the beginnings of dialogue between a country's urban classes.

NGŨGĨ WA THIONG'O
Secret Lives

A new edition of Ngũgĩ's collection of early stories revealing his increased political disillusionment and foreshadowing the novels which have made him one of Africa's foremost commentators.

ALEX LA GUMA
In the Fog of the Seasons' End

This is the story of Beukes – lonely, hunted, determined – working for an illegal organisation, and of Elias Tekwane, captured by the South African police and tortured to death in the cells.

CHARLOTTE BRUNER
The Heinemann Book of African Women's Writing

A companion piece to the earlier *Unwinding Threads*, also edited by Charlotte Bruner, this anthology of writing of the post-colonial era provides new insights into a complex world.

CHINUA ACHEBE & C L INNES
The Heinemann Book of Contemporary African Short Stories

This anthology displays the variety, talent and scope to be found in contemporary African writing. The collection includes work written in English and translations of francophone stories. The magical realism of Kojo Laing and Mia Couto contrasts with the styles of Nadine Gordimer, Ben Okri and Moyez Vassanji.

AMECHI AKWANYA
Orimili

Orimili takes his name from the great river that flows through his home town of Okocha. But while the river flows on to the wider world beyond, Orimili is anchored to his home town, and yearns to push his roots yet further in. His ambition is to be accepted in the company of elders, to wear the thick white thread of office round his ankle.

temporal happiness